W9-BEM-249

For Jimmy —
Mattie says
hi !
Best wishes,
Mary Berger

Mary A. Berger

THE TROUBLE WITH MATTIE

by

Mary A. Berger

Mary A. Berger

The Trouble with Mattie

by

Mary A. Berger

©2010 Mary A. Berger

ALL RIGHTS RESERVED

ISBN: 1453772308
EAN-13: 9781453772300

FIRST EDITION

No part of this book may be used or reproduced in any form or means without the written permission of the author, except in cases of brief quotations.

This is a work of fiction. Names, places, characters, and incidents either are the product of the author's imagination or are used fictitiously, and any resemblance to actual persons, living or dead, business establishments, events, or locales is entirely incidental.

 Dedication

In loving memory of my parents,
Belle and Fred Willett.

Mary A. Berger

Acknowledgements

Many thanks to my husband, Ralph, and my daughters, Jodi and Becky, who keep me supplied with one-liners.

Thanks to Randy Romeo, Attorney at Law, Ron Roberts, my "computer guy," and to Joe Perrone Jr., who edited and designed my book and its cover.

Mary A. Berger

 1

Mattalie Morgan scooted down the dimly lit hallway at Autumn Leaves Housing Center, the swish, swish of her purple jogging suit in rhythm with each step. At the room of her friend, Clare, she pounded on the door.

"Clare, for heaven's sake, open up. It's me, Mattie."

Wearing a muumuu so colorful it looked as if it ran on batteries, a tall, thin woman opened the door. With blushing cheeks and hair the color of flames, her appearance was in sharp contrast to Mattie's petite frame, natural beauty, and dishwater blond hair with its single strand of curl that sometimes hung down over one eye.

Unruffled, Clare greeted her. "Don't tell me, Matts; you found us a suite at the Radisson."

"Yeah, right; complete with two servants and a chauffeur." Mattie brushed her off with a wave of her hand. "Clare, we've got a problem." She whisked by and plunked down onto Clare's favorite lounge chair.

"Come in," Clare said with a smirk, closing the door. "Make yourself comfortable."

Mattie ignored the barb, took a deep breath instead. "Those bullies who supposedly run this place threatened to kick Salina Shaw out."

Clare sat on a footstool opposite Mattie, frowning. "How come?"

"She was going to make waves about them, what a bunch of crooks they are. But Salina called their bluff. She moved out in the middle of the night. Went to her sister's in Virginia. And that reptile, Mr. Reemes, has already leased her room."

Clare propped a hand on one hip. "Well, that's kinda' ballsy."

Mattie picked at a few loose strands of thread on the arm of the chair. "The way Reemes and his flunkies ignore us and hop from one resort to another makes my blood boil." She looked at Clare and quipped, "Is murder still illegal?"

"Maybe not in Detroit," Clare answered with a snicker. Then she grew serious. "There's something wrong with this entire set-up, Mattie." She looked her friend in the eye. "It scares me."

"Well, if you're frightened, think how the others must feel." She looked questioningly at Clare. "So, how'd you ever wind up here?"

"Money. Or lack of it." Clare stared out the window. "I never thought I'd end up in such a miserable—"

"Well, I've only been here a short time," Mattie interrupted, sitting erect, "but I am *so* not liking it. And you should be tired of it, too; everyone here should be. C'mon, Clare, help me think of something we can do, pleeeeze?" Her brow rose, almost pleading, above her slate blue eyes, an acquired expression that she conjured up now and then.

"Not the eyes, Mattie. Don't give me those eyes. And don't go dragging me into another one of your 'causes.'"

Enjoying a mild sense of victory, Mattie nodded toward the back yard. "You mean the kick-the-can game? Wasn't it fun? Got everybody off their rear ends, too," she added proudly.

"Yes, but we almost lost our 'gagateria' privileges that day."

"Our what?"

"Gagateria. You know; the cafeteria—the dining room."

Mattie scoffed, "Big deal. That so-called dining room has as much appeal as a cave."

"Yeah; and there's a rumor that they even add dog food to their casseroles to make them go farther."

"Eeeewww," Mattie squealed, "that's gross!"

Clare simply shrugged. "When we start barking, I'll start worrying."

Mattie shook her head. "I'd call out for a pizza for my next meal if there was a place around here to call," she added dryly. She bolted out of the chair. "Getting back to our problem, if I come up with something I'll let you know."

Clare was grinning. "I'm sure you will."

Back in her little room, Mattie stood before an open window, sipping peppermint tea. Her thoughts turned to that awful day when she'd first arrived there at the center, when she'd felt so helpless and old, instead of her usual energetic, spunky, early-fifty-something self ...

"...I'm not going," Mattie was telling her stepdaughter, Eva.

"But, Mother Mattie, we agreed," protested the dark-haired woman at the wheel of the shiny new black Lincoln. "At your age, a housing center is the best place for you." Her green eyes (usually narrow and cold) grew large with false enthusiasm. "Even Dr. Evans thinks so."

"Dr. Evans?" Mattie came back. "I wouldn't let him work on my dead dog!"

"But the center is such a wonderful place."

"And besides," continued Mattie, on a roll then, "I'm not that old! And I'm certainly not ready for some idiotic *housing* center. And, no, we didn't agree to this; I was told!" Her mouth formed a reticent pout. "I'm not going. And don't you go patronizing me, either, Eva Morgan. Anyone in his right mind could see what you've been up to. Your father passes on, I get laid up with a sprained ankle and the flu, and before I know what's happening, you find a loophole or some foolish thing and steal everything right out from under me!"

Eva had no response.

Mattie let out an impatient sigh. "You know as well as I that there was a new will, Eva. I signed it myself. And it's just a matter of time before they catch up with that imbecile lawyer you're catting around with. Scowling, Mattie stared out the car window. "Some stepdaughter you turned out to be. If I had any sense," she went on, "I'd wrap this cane right around your—"

"Mother Mattie!"

"Don't call me that. Makes my blood boil—what's left of it." Mattie fingered her cane nervously. "I'm beginning to feel like some kind of basket case, being driven off to a wishy-washy *housing* center, while you're all high and mighty—with the money you got from my house." She gripped the cane even tighter.

"You get a monthly allowance," Eva snapped, a smirk crossing her tight face.

"Scraps, you mean." Mattie sighed again, shook her head, and clutched her purse. She'd been taken to the cleaners all right, but her mind was sharp as a blade. Below her fair hair were tender blue eyes that could turn to bolts of lightning. Mattie was known for spouting off, mostly because she enjoyed watching people squirm. And she sometimes used her cane when she felt it appropriate to make a point. The cane, recently acquired but temporary as a result of the sprained ankle, would come in handy.

She sighed and leaned back, staring at the kudzu, mountain laurel, and rolling hills of some place called Farley Gap that passed by outside her window, far from anywhere, out in the hills of western North Carolina. How many more twists and turns could there be before they reached the godforsaken center, wondered Mattie. And why was it so far from everything? Thoughts of her late husband, Gabe, filled her mind. They'd had such a short time together—three years to be exact—before he and Mattie sold their lovely old home and moved from up north to their new rental condo in North Carolina. Of course, without Gabe's income, Mattie had little to live on except for a small pension she received from when she worked. So, she was more or less forced to give up the condo. That's when Eva had stepped in to *help*, and to make arrangements for Autumn Leaves. "Just for now," she had told Mattie, happily aware it was probably all her stepmother could afford at that point.

Mattie gave another sigh. Her thoughts returned once more to those early years with Gabe. Though he was older than Mattie, their years together had been good ones, in spite of her stepdaughter. And he'd adored his "Lovey's" spunk. He'd once told her that he kept her around because she "put zip in his doo-dah."

Eva interrupted Mattie's thoughts. "Don't go to sleep on me now. We're almost there."

"I'd gladly sleep through it," Mattie muttered. As for Eva, Gabe's only offspring, she more or less came with the package when Gabe and Mattie were married. Thanks to Gabe's first wife, a spineless, mousy woman, Eva had been and still was a selfish, manipulating person. Though Mattie tried her best to get along with her, they always seemed to be squabbling.

Eva steered the car into a wide circular drive. Fear and anxiety welled up inside Mattie, and then turned to total foreboding when they pulled in next to the front walk of a faded, sprawling, Low Country cottage.

A dry marble fountain stood in the front yard, flanked by two, rusty wrought iron benches. Beyond that, a great magnolia spread its branches high above a patch of weeds, in the middle of which sat a couple of broken-down yard chairs. Mattie noticed a stream that disappeared into some far off woods. In the distance, she could see the Blue Ridge Mountains, and could just make out the distinctive profile of Mount Pisgah. She swallowed hard.

"...and remember," Eva was promising devoutly, "I'll come visit you every week."

Mattie gave a snort. She'd heard about the month in the Caribbean that Eva had already secretly planned (or so Eva thought). Mattie let out another sigh. It was all happening too fast. If only her wonderful Gabe were still around, everything would be fine. She took a tissue from her purse, and turned away to dab at her eyes while Eva turned off the engine.

"So this is it?" Mattie asked flatly. "You call this wonderful?!" She read aloud from a musty old sign that hung over two large, double doors at the entry, all of which needed either a paint job or complete demolishing—she wasn't sure which. *Autumn Leaves Housing Center For Those In Need*, the sign read. With a sarcastic sniff, she said, "*Autumn Leaves*? Think they'll rake me up and toss me into a trash bag when October comes?"

"Very funny," Eva said, un-amused. She climbed out of the car, went around on Mattie's side, and opened the door for her, a kindness that Mattie was sure she demonstrated only when someone might be watching. A man wearing a white medical coat appeared through the double doors and strutted toward them like he owned the place. Mattie rolled her eyes when he and Eva greeted each other excitedly, especially with Eva's phony enthusiasm. He carried all of Mattie's bags inside, and then returned.

"Good afternoon, Mis' Morgan," the man drawled, turning to Mattie, as she got out of the car. "It's wonderful having y'all with us."

"Yeah, yeah," she said, waving him off, while standing in place just long enough for that unsteady ankle to get stabilized. The medic tried slipping an arm around Mattie's shoulder.

"If you don't mind," she said, pulling back, "I can get around by myself." Instead, the persistent man then tried to pick her up and *carry* her. It was too much for Mattie. Eyes flashing, she drew back her cane and delivered a solid whack to his shinbone. "Outta' my way!" she barked.

With cries of outrage, the medic hopped about on one foot, while holding his injured leg tenderly with one hand. Oblivious, Mattie simply shook her head and started off on her own. Eva, for once at a loss for words, stayed behind to apologize and assist the injured man.

"Hello," a friendly voice said. Mattie looked up to see a young, slender female aide approaching. Her large brown eyes seemed to peek out in delight from long, dark hair. "Y'all must be Mrs. Morgan," she said, smiling. "I'm Lauren Shaw." Her warm, friendly smile widened, even though she kept one eye on Mattie's cane.

Mattie squinted at her. "I like you," she finally announced, offering her arm to the girl. And the two of them strolled inside past some of the residents who'd gathered to see what all the commotion was about, and well ahead of Eva, who was bringing up the rear. "Pinhead," Mattie muttered in her stepdaughter's direction.

Once inside, Lauren introduced Mattie to Mr. Bates, the center's Marketing Officer. He extended his hand to Mattie, who firmed her grip on the cane.

"It's a pleasure, Mrs. Morgan," he said, smiling.

"Hello, Mr. Bates," Mattie said politely, though she felt like spouting: *What kind of place is this? The front yard looks like a bad cemetery and this building reminds me of a tomb! Why not just call it, End of the Road Burial Grounds?* Instead, she responded with an unexpected question. "Do you folks have inspectors here?" She caught the quick glance between Mr. Bates and Lauren, even though the question went unanswered. Regardless, she seemed to take a liking to Mr. Bates, so she softened her grip on the cane. "Actually, I'd like to go to my room and get out of these shoes. I need a cup of tea."

Mr. Bates looked relieved. "I think we can arrange that."

Eva and the wounded medic arrived on the scene, her face flushing with rage when she spotted Mattie. On seeing Mr. Bates, however, her expression brightened. "Mr. Bates...Harold," she said, giving a silly laugh, "how nice to see you again." She placed her hand on his arm, while a blush of embarrassment crept up his neck. Mattie caught his look of discomfort and smiled to herself.

The angry medic turned to Mr. Bates. "Just look at this!" he spouted, hiking up his pant leg. A good-sized welt appeared on his leg from Mattie's cane. "We can't tolerate this sort of thing here, Mr. Bates," he spouted, glaring at Mattie. "What do y'all suggest we do?"

Harold Bates leaned forward and looked at the injury with sympathetic concern. "You might try using some ice."

Without another word, Mattie and Lauren went wandering off together. Eva followed on their heels, flinging the tails of her rabbit skin furs over a shoulder.

There was a new commander at the helm of Autumn Leaves, as Eva issued orders right-and-left, and argued with Lauren.

"Now, Mother Mattie, Dear," Eva said as they stood together at the door to Mattie's room. "This is for the best; you'll see. They tell me there are wonderful programs here." She forced a smile, glancing over at Lauren.

It was all Mattie could do to put up with Eva's patronizing tone and glorified stories about how great it was going to be. To Mattie, everything looked so gloomy that she was sure the place must be run by mummies.

"This isn't the end, Eva," she said, eyes blazing. "Jed Mitchell will get to the bottom of everything sooner or later." She moved her cane so that the tip of it stopped just short of her stepdaughter's foot. "He's a lawyer, Eva, and a good one. He'll take care of you."

Eva stiffened, then adjusted her furs, and gathered her handbag. "Well, this is the way things are, *Mother Mattie,*" she added sarcastically before leaving.

"Enjoy your Caribbean cruise," Mattie called after her, her sarcasm weak compared to the anger she felt inside.

On hearing Mattie's words, Eva's pace faltered and she missed a step. Her look of genuine surprise when she glanced back was priceless to Mattie. Then, with an arrogant toss of her head, Eva squared her shoulders, turned, and walked away. "Hope the boat sinks," Mattie muttered to herself.

Glancing around at her new surroundings, Mattie was filled with a sudden rush of despair at how drab and dull everything in the little room appeared. Plain walls of grey greeted her; dark brown carpet, badly soiled, stared up at her. She turned to Lauren and said testily, "I hope these bright colors don't blind me."

"Want to borrow my sunglasses?" retorted Lauren. Mattie liked that, and chuckled. "I'll bring you some tea," the aide offered.

"Thank you, dear. I'm just going to take a short walk after I get into my 'tennies.'"

"Yes, ma'am."

Strolling in the hall, Mattie noticed to her dismay that all the residents' doors were closed. On the walls hung only a couple of faded prints of mountain scenes. She noticed an old-fashioned light fixture with one of its bulbs missing. "It's like a B movie," she muttered.

Turning back, she heard a door opening across the hall. "That was quite a scene," a cynical voice said.

Mattie looked over to see a tall, older woman standing in the doorway. She had on a garish green and fuchsia flowered muumuu. Mattie frowned at the dyed orange-red color of her hair. "Excuse me?" she asked.

"You. Outdoors, with your cane, and that ass of a medic."

News travels fast, Mattie thought. "Oh, that. That was just—"

"And who was the broad with the fake furs?" Mattie gave the woman a questioning look and watched her swirl some ice cubes in the glass of amber liquid she held. "We sure don't see many like her around here," the woman said with a chuckle, before extending her hand. "I'm Clare. Clare Tibbitts."

Though Clare appeared to be much older than Mattie was, it was hard to tell, with the gaudy makeup job, dark eyeliner, shiny eye shadow, and heavy blush. "Well, it's nice to meet you, Clare. Lived here long?"

"Too long," Clare responded dryly.

From down the hall, another female voice cut in. "But you get used to it after a while."

"There isn't enough liquor," Clare said dryly. "You never really get used to being here, Mattie. You just curl up and die of boredom."

Mattie didn't like the sound of that. *Die of boredom?* Not Mattie. Never. She'd have to show them that!

Mary A. Berger

 2

Mattie's thoughts were interrupted when a breeze popped the curtain nearby. A shaft of sunlight slid through, melting on her skin. She took another sip of her tea—the peppermint so soothing and comforting.

The tea seemed almost to save her life; things were so dreary there, including her own room. Despite its bleak appearance, there was a mini-refrigerator and a small stove, with an oven and two burners—lifesavers, both of them. A couple of double-hung windows let in the only daylight. A lounge chair, an old television, a small dinner table with two chairs, a twin bed, and a tiny bathroom completed the package.

Her thoughts turned to her pals, "playing" kick-the-can outdoors there at the center, and the wonderful time they'd had! It warmed her insides, since the bigwigs seemed to frown on people having fun—all except them.

"We have to do something about this," she murmured, sipping more of her tea.

Even so, Mattie didn't want anyone to end up like Salina Shaw, on the spot, forced to put up or shut up, even though Mattie was certain she, herself, would be out of there soon.

The fact that Gabe's will was missing ate away at her. "I saw Gabe put our wills in the safe," she had told Jed Mitchell, their "up north" attorney, who had come right down as soon as he heard about Gabe. "In fact," she went on, "all our private papers are gone! I can't help feeling that Eva's responsible." Jed frowned in disgust at the idea, as

Mattie continued. "But would she go that far; steal important papers right out from under our noses? And how could she get away with it?!"

"Mattie," the secretly adoring Jed said, putting a warm hand on her shoulder, "we'll get to the bottom of this, I promise." His voice sounded reassuring and caring. "I've already got someone working on it." His soft blue eyes looked into hers. "Try to bear up, please."

"But what about our North Carolina lawyer, Owen Black, who drew up our wills here?" Mattie asked him. "He was supposed to be a good lawyer, from what we were told. Where is he? And what's his part in all of this?"

"I wish I knew. At this point, we just don't have that much information."

"Well, all I know is I'm stuck here in this dump, and I don't know what to do." Her voice began to crack, and she reached for a tissue and dabbed at her eyes as the tears welled.

Jed drew her into his arms and held her while she cried. "I'm so sorry, Mattie. You don't deserve any of this."

Regaining her composure, Mattie stepped back, sniffing, and said with a huge sigh, "Thank God you're helping me, Jed."

Now, as she finished her tea, Mattie recalled that conversation and how grateful she'd felt to Jed. She truly didn't know what she'd have done without his help.

As for her present circumstances, Mattie had begun asking more questions about the housing center. Who were its owners? Why hadn't she met them? Of course, she'd been introduced to Mr. Bates and had met Mr. Reemes, whatever *his* position was, when he'd gotten after her about the outdoors game "Not allowed!" he'd stormed. But as far as she could see, there was no one else in charge. In fact, she had seen Mr. Bates only once since her first day, and that was from a distance.

To Mattie, the strangest part was why the center itself was in such shambles. She planned to do some "nosing around" on her own. There hadn't been any signs of physical abuse, thank goodness. But it seemed to her that most of the residents she'd spoken with felt second-rate, as if they didn't matter; yet all were apparently thankful just to have a place to call home, even though "home" was somewhere out in the sticks. Mattie cringed at the thought of being under someone's thumb this way for the rest of her life. Still, she was mystified: How could the authorities not do anything about these morbid surroundings?

And worse, how did Eva find this place and get her into it, without so much as talking with her about it first?! Mattie had just been told: this is where you're going. Period. Even Jed Mitchell was bewildered, and very concerned.

Mattie gave a shudder, then zipped up the jacket of her jogging suit, and headed for the lobby to go outside. Being outdoors always made her feel better, especially now that her ankle had healed, and she no longer needed the cane.

Approaching the front desk, which was always unoccupied, she glanced around. "What's this?" she muttered, spying a certificate that hung on the wall nearby. She hadn't noticed it before and leaned closer to get a better look. It was a certificate of approval, with the state's name and this year's date!

She shook her head in disbelief and muttered, "How can this be?" Then from across the hall, she heard a door open and saw a distinguished looking man come out, lock the door, then walk away with the spoilsport, Mr. Reemes, at his side. They hadn't noticed Mattie until Reemes turned and spotted her. His icy glare sent a slight chill through her bones. She wondered what they had locked up in there. Probably troublemakers like me, she told herself.

The other man looked important to Mattie. In spite of her misgivings, she knew she had to find out who he was. With their backs to her as they walked away, she sneaked up behind them, and faked a misstep, which threw her into a slight collision with the distinguished looking man. Of course, she apologized profusely and, while ignoring the cold stare from Mr. Reemes, introduced herself.

"Hello," she said, extending her hand. "I'm Mrs. Mattalie Morgan. You can call me Mattie."

The man stiffened a bit but still kept his somewhat dignified manner. "Hello, Mrs. Morgan. I'm Mr. Prescott. Wynn Prescott." They shook hands and he started to introduce her to Mr. Reemes.

"Oh, I know who he is," Mattie said with a wave of her hand. Of course, her idea was to take advantage of the situation, so she quickly asked, "Exactly what do you do here, Mr. Prescott?"

With a guarded smile, he answered. "I . . . own Autumn Leaves." On hearing that, Mattie didn't waste a moment. "Say, do you suppose we could have a little chat some day? I've got some things on my mind that might interest you." Momentarily taken aback, Mr. Prescott hesitated, then replied, "Er, sure. We'll do that some day."

"When?" Mattie asked bluntly.

With a self-conscious and urge-to-kill laugh, Mr. Reemes interrupted and told Mattie, "Look, we have things to tend to right now, Mrs. Morgan. Perhaps another day."

They brushed her off, while he rescued Mr. Prescott from the possibility of a showdown with her.

Mattie grinned to herself, took a pencil and piece of paper from her pocket, and jotted down the name of Wynn Prescott.

As she turned and headed toward the two, front double-doors to go outside, she heard a man's nasal-sounding voice. "Hey there, bee-yoo-tee-ful," he said. When she looked, there was a small, skinny guy blocking her way. His floral shirt, unbuttoned to the waist, revealed a bunch of tarnished gold chains that were draped across his bony chest. Under a silly looking straw hat, a section of hair hung from an obvious toupee. He flashed a crooked smile. "Goin' my way?" he asked suggestively.

"I doubt it," Mattie replied, drawing back.

When she tried to maneuver around the man, he stepped in front of her again. "How about giving my heart a jump-start?"

"You'd need open heart surgery, when I got through with you!" Mattie spouted. "Now get outta' my way!"

At once, he shrank, shoulders slumping, and lost his smile. As he turned away, Mattie heard him whining, "They never wanna cooperate. Always giving me a hard time!"

She gave a snicker and came close to feeling sorry for the guy.

Mattie finally made it outside. She paused beneath the robin's egg sky to breathe in the spring air, heavy with the scent of lilacs from a single bush that had somehow survived, obviously without care. The aroma made her feel alive.

Just then, she heard someone calling to her as Clare caught up. "Hey, Matts, did you hear about Fae Munn? She had a stroke!"

"A stroke? But she's only, what? Forty, forty-five years old?" Mattie thought a moment, and then recalled Fae as a worrywart at her kick-the-can outing. She could see Fae timidly joining in, yet shrinking back when the game got rowdy. "Well, that's too bad. How's she doing?"

"Not good. Without the right therapy, poor Fae can barely move." Clare saw Mattie's concern. "They had her in a hospital for a few days, but she was sent back here. Something about insurance. I guess she has a therapist now and then, but . . ."

Mattie couldn't believe there was no one properly tending to the woman. "Maybe we can help," she told Clare. "C'mon, let's go see her."

Just then, something in the yard caught Mattie's eye. A woman in overalls was chasing a darting puppy that was zigzagging across the yard. Mattie assumed they were from a nearby farm.

Then Mattie remembered an Oreo she'd put in her pocket earlier. She nudged Clare. "Watch this."

She went out to the yard, sat down, and held the Oreo in her outstretched palm. The pup came right over. While he downed the cookie, Mattie got a firm grip on his collar.

The breathless, laughing woman caught up and thanked her. "Scooter" let Mattie pet him, his coat satiny-soft to her touch. There was something soothing, almost therapeutic about petting a dog.

Suddenly, Mattie's eyes sizzled. She turned to the woman and said, "Could I ask a favor of you?"

Back inside the center, Clare and Mattie walked side by side, both silent and straight-faced. No one noticed the squirming bulge beneath Mattie's jacket. When they approached the corner to Fae's room, Mattie stood back while Clare checked to see if the hall was clear. There'd almost certainly be another scolding if word got out that they had a dog inside the center, especially after all the "trouble" Mattie had caused with the yard game. She rolled her eyes at that.

Clare waved an okay, and Mattie scooted into Fae's room, while Clare stood guard at the door. Patting her jacket, Mattie warned, "Scooter, you know the rules: no pets are allowed here so you'd better behave or we'll be down the tubes."

She opened her jacket, let out the wriggling mass of black fur, and turned to Fae. "Fae; it's Mattie." Fae's only response was an empty stare. Mattie set the puppy on the bed, reached for Fae's limp hand, and gently placed it on the dog. "I brought someone with me. He's a puppy and he's full of you-know-what." She backed away and sat in a nearby chair, while giving Scooter a final order: "And don't you go peeing on that bed!"

Oddly enough, the pup settled down with Fae's hand still in place, and nestled close. To Mattie, they seemed an unlikely pair: Fae helpless, Scooter filled with "puppyness."

The dog turned and licked Fae's hand. All at once, Mattie thought she saw something. Yes, Fae's hand moved. There, it moved again! "Well, what d'you know," she murmured. Then she couldn't believe what she saw; a single tear spilled from Fae's eye and trickled down her cheek. Mattie didn't know whether to laugh or cry. All she was certain of was this moment, this peaceful moment, nothing more.

Later Mattie and Clare returned the puppy to its waiting owner, Jean, who promised to let them "borrow" Scooter again soon, as she gave each of the women her phone number. "Call any time," she told them.

Then Mattie and Clare strolled back across the grounds toward the center. A strong breeze swept a couple of redbuds, their leaves rustling like raised hopes. Mattie sighed. In spite of her own circumstances, she tried to hold a positive outlook. "Isn't it wonderful, just to be alive?" she said to Clare. Then she stopped abruptly and pointed in the distance. "Look, it's so clear today you can see Mt. Pisgah. Look, Clare!"

Clare stopped and enjoyed the view. Then she grew thoughtful. "But you know we'll get in trouble. About the dog, I mean. Someone's bound to squeal."

Mattie gave a little snort. "Who cares? Besides, we can't just stick our heads in the sand, or give up." Her chin jutted out as if to emphasize her point. "We can't ever give up."

"I'll make a poster with those exact words and pass it around," Clare said sarcastically.
Mattie came to an abrupt halt, her eyes suddenly aglow. "Clare, that's it! We'll make flyers! And we'll get a petition going."

Clare gawked. "Flyers? Petition? What for?"

"To stir up the folks. Look, Clare, I know the people who live here are in need, and have only this sad place to call their home, but why do they have to live like...well...like losers?" Mattie's words were heartfelt and sincere. And Clare didn't have an answer.

Mattie waved a cautious finger. "But we can't get caught doing any of this," she said, referring to the flyers. She knew the idea could be risky, but it didn't matter to her right now; the high spirits she felt at this moment would see her through anything.

Mattie headed off on her own, spouting her plan, as if no one else were around. "We'll talk to Harry, that goofy mail clerk. I can con him out of some paper and markers." She glanced back at her friend. "Come on, Clare; keep up."

Clare snickered but, like an obedient child, tagged along while "Matts" went on. "We'll sneak out in the middle of the night, and slide the flyers underneath everyone's doors." Clare laughed out loud at that. "We should plan a rally," Mattie went on. "We can have it at my place." And the two of them continued on their way, giggling like schoolgirls over Mattie's ideas.

Later on that day, when suppertime rolled around, Mattie wandered into the dining room with its dull grey carpet, threadbare in places, and soiled with food stains. She cringed, as usual, at the grease-spotted, brown print wallpaper, its corners tearing away. A couple of dull chandeliers dangled from the ceiling. Mattie let out another sigh, and thought glumly, *How can any of us even begin to enjoy a meal here?*

Just then, one of the residents passed by carrying a small food tray. "Chicken Fricassee" the menu taped on the wall said. When Mattie saw the food, she squealed, "Eeeewww!" One glance reminded her of something she'd once seen in a test tube, and it set her off. "This is appalling!" she cried out to no one in particular.

A server, who was dishing out gravy, stopped dishing in mid-air, and gave Mattie a disinterested, "So?"

"I refuse to eat one more meal here!" Mattie announced for all the room to hear. There was total silence.

All eyes were on her, as the server said, "Hey, I know it ain't very cheerful but—"

"Cheerful?!" Mattie exploded. "Cheerful like the county morgue! When do the dead bodies start rolling by?" She started back to her room, when the aide Lauren showed up, just in time to hear the end of Mattie's outburst. "Mrs. Morgan," she said; "wait!"

"From now on," Mattie informed her calmly, "I'll have my meals at my place."

Back in her room, Mattie paced the floor. Her teakettle was on, and the pacing gave her something to do until it whistled. She asked herself, over and over, *What am I doing here? What has happened to my life?* Close to tears, she reminded herself that the only thing keeping her going was the knowledge that Jed Mitchell was helping her with the estate. She had been waiting anxiously each day to hear from him again.

After making tea, Mattie was about to sink into her chair, when she heard a tap at her door, which she had closed (unusual for Mattie). She didn't want to talk to anyone right then, and ignored it. At the second tap, however, she couldn't help herself. "Who's there?"

"It's Lauren. May I come in?" Mattie just couldn't turn her away.

"Of course, Lauren. You're always welcome." Mattie was taken by surprise as Lauren walked in carrying a dinner tray. The tray held two small bowls of vegetable soup and a cheese sandwich cut in half.

Lowering her voice, Lauren said, "Now don't y'all tell a soul, but this is my supper that I brought from home. I thought you might be hungry. Think maybe we could share it?"

Mattie didn't know what to say. Slowly, she smiled her appreciation. "That would be nice. Thank you, Lauren. Come in. We'll have supper together."

Just then, they heard Lauren being paged over the intercom. Lauren sagged. "I'm sorry, I can't stay," she said. "They're calling me." She handed the tray to Mattie. "If I'm not back shortly, go ahead and have my share. I'll grab something later."

Mattie took the tray, and thanked Lauren once more. Her spirits lifted by Lauren's kindly gesture, she sat back in her chair, enjoying the soup, and thought about Gabe.

Later, Mattie began wondering about her friends back home, how none of them had called or been by to see her, after sincere promises. Actually, her telephone had rung only twice since she'd lived there, both calls from Jed Mitchell.

"There's nothing to do," she moaned with a sigh. Aside from the outdoors game and the idea of the flyers, Mattie still felt bored. There wasn't even any trouble to get into at Autumn Leaves, not any *real* trouble, at least. However, she reminded herself with a smile, the folks did seem to go for her kick-the-can outing.

The next morning, Mattie put on a yellow tee shirt with matching sweats, and her "tennies." "I feel sunny and bright," she told her reflection in the mirror. After her exercises and a brisk walk, Mattie had the urge to go exploring. Lauren had told her there once was a small greenhouse somewhere on the grounds out back. Just the thought of it made Mattie's "green thumbs" itch. She was determined to find it.

In the hall, she met Clare. "Oh, Clare, come with me," Mattie said, explaining that she was headed out back to find the greenhouse. "You probably weren't doing anything anyway. Come with me and help me find it, pleeeze?"

Clare stopped in her tracks, her eyes popping open wide. "Girl, are you *nuts*? You don't know there's a greenhouse back there. Besides, there could be a mass murderer hanging out in those woods."

"Duhhh," Mattie said, and showed Clare a chain she was wearing around her neck, with a large whistle attached. "I've got my safety whistle with me, just as a precaution."

Clare slumped. "I don't know, Mattie. It's just—"

"Okay, then. How about this: What if I promise to get you a bottle of rum or whatever it is you like to drink; then will you go with me?" After seeing Clare's look of relenting, Mattie added, "You don't have anything better to do, and you know it."

"You got me there," Clare said with a shrug, followed by a big sigh. "Oh, all right, as long as I get my rum reward."

Mattie muttered aside, "Geez, now I have to bribe her to cooperate."

Stepping out onto the back porch they noticed three women sitting in some rickety porch chairs. Mattie called to them. "Hi, ladies. I remember you from the game outside."

Smiling, the one called Lillian said, "And we all remember you, Mattie!" They exchanged greetings and Lillian asked, "Mattie, when are we gonna do something else that's fun? We need you to get us going."

Mattie smiled mischievously. "You'll see what I've got cooked up very soon."

"Good," Kathy said; "that'll give us somethin' to do. I've been waitin' for my friends from Charlotte to come and see me but, honey, they ain't showed up yet."

"Yeah, me too," Lillian said. "Since I was forced to come out here to Autumn Leaves, I figured I'd be near some friends, but I haven't seen them once!"

"Probably because they can't *find* you," Mattie told them with a snicker.

"Y'know, you're getting to be pretty famous around here," Kathy told Mattie, who scoffed good-naturedly, "Well, I do like to keep things moving."

"She means me," Clare said. "I can't go out of my room without her chasing me down. She's like the Mounted Police; always on my trail!"

The others laughed, but the one called Gwen just got up and walked away without a word. Mattie shrugged at the others. They exchanged knowing looks and Lillian said, "Don't pay no attention to Gwen, Mattie. She's kinda (Lillian opened her mouth and stuck a finger in it, pretending to gag) if you get my drift."

"Lord above," Mattie muttered before they said their good-byes, and she and Clare continued on their way.

Heading out back of the grounds of Autumn Leaves, Mattie paused to take in a breath of fresh spring air, luscious with the perfume of apple blossoms from a nearby tree. "It's great just to be outside, isn't it, Clare?"

Clare had to agree. "You know, Mattie, I've heard that Autumn Leaves owns several acres here and that the property goes back even beyond the woods."

"Really?"

While they strolled along chatting, Mattie mentioned the odd guy she ran into the other day who tried to block her way at the front door.

"Oh, you must mean Bernard," Clare said. He thinks he's a lady-killer. He's okay, but..." She paused. "Well...his wheel's turning, but the hamster's gone, if you know what I mean." Mattie let out a loud squawk of a laugh. "In fact," Clare confessed, "I once actually had a date with him, just for kicks."

"A date? Where'd you go?"

"We just walked up the road. Took our lunch and found an old, broken down picnic table."

"I can't imagine that," Mattie said, not really believing her story. "Well, tell me how your date was with that creep?"

"He's aggressively slow. All he did was rub my knee."

"Lucky you!" Mattie said, then she added, "But, Clare, it's not that I just don't like him . . ." She paused, and then shook her head. "Nah, I just don't like him."

Clare snickered, and then changed the subject. "By the way, I've been meaning to ask, what about the flyers and stuff? Any more 'dirty work' up your sleeve?"

"Not yet. I've been to the mailroom a few times, but Harry's never around. Don't worry; I'll get the stuff we need."

Clare smiled to herself, knowing that if Mattie said she would, she would.

Further on, they came to a stand of tall weeds, intermixed with rhododendron and mountain laurel. Looking closer, Mattie noticed some rusty metal protruding from the top of one of the tall bushes. Her curiosity got the better of her. "C'mon, Clare; let's have a look."

Cautiously, the women tried to forge a path through the brush. Some of the rhododendron and mountain laurel had grown together so tightly that their branches were heavily intertwined and gnarled, forming an almost jungle-like growth.

"How're we going to get through this mess?" Mattie moaned.

"Here, maybe this will help," Clare said, reaching into the pocket of her muumuu. Mattie watched in surprise as Clare pulled out a good-sized switchblade knife, easily

26

flicked out a long, razor-sharp blade and began hacking at some of the taller weeds.

Mattie looked astonished. "Where'd you get that? Steal it from the Grim Reaper?"

"You've got your whistle; I've got this," Clare said without missing a weed.

Moving closer, they could see jagged pieces of glass attached to some metal where whole glass panels had once been.

"What the ?" Mattie muttered, craning her neck.

"Careful, Mattie," Clare cautioned. "Remember: mass murderers."

The women stood before a metal doorframe. Mattie nudged it. The door swung back. Suddenly, she hollered, "Yikes!" and jumped for her life, when a long black snake slithered by.

They both screamed and ran from the place, scaring out a couple of mockingbirds that flapped their wings overhead.

"Yikes!" Mattie gasped again, clutching her heart, which was beating faster than the speed of sound.

"Whew! That was close!" Clare said, panting.

"Lord above!" Mattie said, almost in a whisper.

Once safely out of the brush, Mattie turned back to take another look and noticed a vertical pipe. Her eyes followed it up to the top, where a corroded sprinkler was attached. Her mouth fell open. "Clare, look over there," she said, slumping. "So this was the greenhouse." Her heart sank in disappointment. "I had hoped to find something more." She let out a dejected sigh, shrugged and the two of them headed back to the center.

When they got there, Clare wanted to go visit Fae and see if any progress had been made since her stroke. Mattie said she had to use the bathroom, so she told Clare she'd catch up with her later. Actually, Mattie just wanted the time to herself. Overcome with disappointment about the greenhouse, she plopped into her chair and gazed out the window. She had so hoped to find at least a semblance of a structure; instead, all she found was the barest, most disappointing remnant.

"If only" she said aloud with a sigh, "if only there had been more to it, I would've gone out there and picked things up myself, anything to give me something to do, or a place to go." She gave a shrug. "I guess there's no point in thinking about it now...unless..."

Suddenly, Mattie's eyes brightened. "I wonder if there's a maintenance man or groundskeeper somewhere?" she muttered, though deep inside she doubted such a person existed. Autumn Leaves had provided no brochures or information about any of the staff, so there really was no way of looking up a name or making a phone call. She wondered what would happen if a resident got hurt or needed medical help. The thought made her uneasy.

Mattie heard someone tapping at her open door. "Mrs. Morgan, I'm on a break for a few minutes." It was Lauren. "How about some of that tea of yours?"

"Wonderful!" Mattie responded, perking up when she saw the woman. "But let's take it outside and sit on the porch, okay?"

They had the porch all to themselves. Once they were situated, Lauren asked, "Mrs. Morgan, you've never said, but do you have any family?"

"Only Scotty. My deceased cousin's boy, but I call him my nephew." Mattie's expression brightened when she mentioned him. "He's up in Cleveland, where my husband

and I lived before we came here. Nice young man, a whiz at computers," she added, "fun to be around."

Lauren took a swallow of tea. "What brought y'all down here?"

"My husband liked the four seasons," Mattie told her, "which is why we ended up renting a condo in the mountains near Asheville." Then Mattie began telling her about the old Morgan homestead up north. "It was all refurbished and updated by my husband, who was a builder," she said. "There were wooden plantation blinds and velour draperies at the windows. Then, there was a beautiful carved oak staircase that began outside the front parlor and curved its way to the upper level. Actually," she said, leaning forward, "there were three levels, not counting the attic. And, Lauren, I wish you could have seen the old things in that attic!"

"Like what?"

"Oh, like old birdcages, brass bed frames, lots of old side tables and clocks and, well, I could go on forever." She set her teacup down. "But, the octagon shaped sunroom, ah, that was my favorite spot! The late afternoon sun would come streaming in through a huge bay window, and parts of the windows were faceted so that when the sun shone on the facets, they'd reflect on the oak floor in all shades of the rainbow! Absolutely gorgeous!"

Lauren smiled and took some more of her tea. "But wasn't it hard to go from a beautiful old home like that to a condominium?"

"Oh, at first I missed it terribly." Mattie said, smiling. "But actually, our condo was almost as big as that old house! And we were only renting it temporarily. But, Lauren, when you love someone, you don't care if you're living in the desert! Besides," she continued wistfully,

"Gabe was having health problems and wasn't expected to live long. He wanted to take an early retirement and he wanted the mountains. So this is where we came."

Lauren listened thoughtfully, finishing her tea.

Mattie's expression changed. "Oh, then there's Eva. My stepdaughter."

"The woman who brought you here?"

"*Dumped* is more like it." Mattie said, looking away. "Some day I'll tell you the whole story, Lauren; some day." Then, out of the blue, and changing the subject, Mattie blurted, "What happened to that greenhouse? Why wasn't it kept up?"

Lauren looked surprised. "You mean the one they say was out by the woods? Y'all actually found it?!"

"Bingo!"

"What were you doing all the way out there?"

"Oh, just 'snoopuh' exploring."

"All by *yourself?*"

"Clare was with me. Besides, when I walk very far," Mattie assured her, "I wear my whistle around my neck." She didn't mention Clare's butcher knife, and quickly went back to talking about the greenhouse. "Whatever happened to it, anyway?"

Lauren shrugged. "No one's ever asked."

"Well, someone has now," Mattie informed her, downing the last of her tea. "It's such a waste! And dangerous, too. Broken glass everywhere. Someone could get hurt."

Lauren leaned forward, looking right at her. "Yes, someone like you!" She glanced at her watch. "I've got to get back. I'm the only one on duty today. Oh, by the way, since y'all enjoy plants so much, a speaker's coming out next week to talk about plants and gardening, and stuff. I'll let you know when. Y'all interested?"

Mattie's jaw dropped. "You mean there actually are *programs* here? Sure, I'll come."

Mary A. Berger

 3

It rained all day the next day, so Mattie curled up with a book she'd ignored for several days. She loved mysteries, especially legal suspense. But when she got to a part about a woman who'd lost her husband, she couldn't go on. She sat staring out her window and fell into a dark mood. Maybe it was the rain. Maybe it was just being where she was. And, of course, she still missed Gabe.

Autumn Leaves was a far cry from the old Morgan homestead that Mattie had grown to love before they decided to sell it and move to Asheville. Thoughts of that old homestead reminded her of the early days when she and Gabe had first met. She'd worked in the office of a large landscaping company on the outskirts of Cleveland. One day, Gabe had simply rushed in, and after greeting a few of her co-workers, approached Mattie, and introduced himself.

"Well, Mattie," he said, after some small talk, "how would you like to come with me and see my new place?" He glanced over at Sarah, her boss. "You don't mind if I steal this gal away for a while, do you, Sarah? It's close to quitting time, anyway." Without waiting for Sarah's okay, he nearly dragged Mattie away from her desk, he was that excited.

Mattie gave her boss a questioning look. "It's alright, Mattie. He's safe."

Gabe laughed loudly. "What a thing to say about a good man like me: safe." Smiling, he helped Mattie with her jacket, and the two of them left in a hurry. Mattie had no idea he'd been waiting for the opportunity to take her out. Or that he'd even said something to Sarah ahead of time that he'd like to date "that gorgeous girl."

An independent builder, Gabe had just completed the restoration of his old Victorian style mansion out in the rolling country near Seven Hills, and he wanted her to see it. "And give me some landscaping tips," he'd added, as if to keep things credible.

Tall, tanned, dark-haired, Gabe was a widower and much older than Mattie. The two of them chatted in the car all the way out to the house, and of course she fell in love with it—and with him. Mattie smiled as she recalled the day they were married just a few months later.

Dressed in an off-white, knee-length, silk brocade dress with long sleeves, she looked ravishing, as some of the guests told her. Gabe sported a red bow tie with his navy suit and, to Mattie, appeared suave and handsome. Even Scotty, her nephew, wore a suit.

"This is the first time I've ever seen you dressed up," Mattie told him. "You look wonderful!"

"Yeah, but I can't wait to get out of this," Scotty came back, tugging at his collar. "But since it's for you, Aunt Mattie…"

"Oh, that's so sweet," she said, bending his arm backwards playfully and putting him in a hammer lock.

Of course, he faked a cry of "abuse!" and they ended up laughing and hugging.

The ceremony had taken place in her favorite spot, the octagon sunroom, in the newly refurbished homestead, surrounded by all their friends, including Jed Mitchell, their attorney, with the sunlight streaming in through the windows, Gabe's arms wrapped lovingly around her, and him murmuring his pet name for her: Lovey…

Mattie fell asleep with a smile on her face.

The next day Mattie got busy caring for the few plants she had. Using a small watering can, she went to a philodendron, then to an ivy, and finally a Boston fern that hung near her window. She had found some cord and a nail in her "junk" drawer and used them to hang the fern. Her pride and joy, a white violet, bloomed on top of her little table.

She was just finishing up when she heard a tap on her door. "Come on in. Door's open. Have time for some tea?" she asked without looking, thinking it was probably Clare.

"Hello, Mattie," a man's voice said.

"Hey, good-looking," came the voice of another younger male.

Mattie whirled around as the watering can fell from her hands. "Jed! Scotty! What a wonderful surprise!" She scooted across the room into the waiting arms of her closest friend and "up north" lawyer, Jed Mitchell, a ruddy-faced, pleasant man whose friendly grey-blue eyes held a special gleam for Mattie.

Her nephew, Scotty, let out an unrestrained howl of pleasure, as he hoisted her up off the floor in his big strong arms and swung her around.

"Put me down, you young fool!" she protested, loving every minute, and he kissed her with a loud smack on the cheek. Mattie straightened her shirt and dabbed at her eyes with a tissue. "You need a haircut," she let him know, noticing his shoulder-length, sun bleached hair. "And what's that say on your t-shirt?" She leaned closer. "'Mr. Wonderful'." She shook her head. "Scotty, you'll never change."

"Neither will you."

She swatted him playfully on the seat of his blue jeans.

"Sit, sit, sit," she chirped, and directed them to a couple of chairs. "We'll have tea. Jed take off that jacket and be comfortable."

Jed shook his head and began apologizing. "I'm so sorry, Mattie; we can't stay. Have to catch a flight back to Cleveland. But I wanted to at least stop by and keep in touch."

Mattie's disappointment showed. "Oh, that's too bad. I always look forward so much to seeing you."

"You look wonderful, Mattie," Jed told her, that special gleam showing in his warm eyes.

"I feel wonderful, except...well, you know the story. It's enough to make me come unglued."

Jed grew thoughtful. "I have some news about your estate." Mattie's eyes opened wide.

"I have people helping us."

"That's good. What have they come up with?"

"Well, we're trying to find Eva and that lawyer boyfriend of hers." Jed looked serious. "Mattie, about that lawyer..." He took her hand in his. "You recall when you and Gabe moved here and had your wills drawn up by Owen Black?"

She nodded. "Yes, our North Carolina lawyer."

Jed looked deep in her eyes. "Mattie...he's Eva's boyfriend."

Shocked, Mattie drew in a deep breath. "What?!" For a moment, she was speechless. When it sank in what Jed had just told her, she said, "I knew Eva was running around with some lawyer, but I didn't know who!" She shook her head. "I can't believe it. I was aware that Owen had just been divorced, but I didn't think he was desperate."

36

"Remember when Eva moved down here," Jed went on, "and took that waitress job at the diner?" Mattie nodded. "Well, she went to see Owen Black for some 'legal' issues right away, as soon as she learned he was going to be drawing up your wills. According to Owen's secretary, Eva threw herself at him and, within days, the two of them became an item."

Mattie's eyes grew larger with each part of Jed's news. "And now you can't find either one of them?!" She gave a sarcastic sniff. "Maybe they fell overboard on the cruise ship." Still bewildered, she said, "I knew there was something about that guy that didn't sit right with me."

Giving Mattie's hand a gentle squeeze, Jed sounded reassuring. "Try not to worry," he said affectionately; "I know we'll find them." Then he changed the subject. "Er, Mattie, you do get a pension from when you worked in an office, don't you?"

"A very small one. That and the monthly *allowance* that Eva told me I'd be getting. It helps me out a little. I order some stuff when Lauren works here and when she goes to the nearest burg and picks up my tea and food and a few other things." She chuckled softly. "Almost makes me wish I was old enough for Social Security."

"And it's too bad Gabe wasn't," Jed said.

"I know. He just missed it by a couple of months."

With a sigh of frustration, Jed said, "Believe me, Mattie, we will get to the bottom of all this." His voice grew deep as he spoke, and there was more than warm admiration for her in his eyes.

"I know, Jed, I know. It's just that everything happened so fast. II still can't believe I'm here in this God-forsaken place with no car, no condo. I mean, who would've thought?" Her voice began to crack.

"You mustn't blame yourself or Gabe for anything," Jed told her tenderly, taking her hands in his. "Just believe that everything will be all right."

She looked fondly at him, smiled and said, "Jed, you should have one of those T-shirts like Scotty's wearing," nodding at the Mr. Wonderful logo. A warm blush then filled her cheeks and forced her to turn away.

Jed checked his watch and reminded Scotty of their schedule. They all exchanged hugs and bid each other good-bye. "We'll be in touch, Mattie," Jed assured her. "And very soon."

Mattie waited at the door to her room until they were out of sight, then started back inside.

"Hey-y-y. Not bad." It was Clare from across the hall. She'd apparently been standing in her doorway for some time, but Mattie hadn't noticed. "Two men! And good-looking ones. How do you do it, Mattie?" she teased, sipping the drink she held.

"Well, I don't mean to brag," Mattie came back, "but when you're hot, you're hot."

Looking down at her somewhat flat chest and sagging muumuu, Clare answered, "And when you're not, you're not."

Back in her room, Mattie sat in her chair and gazed out the window, overwhelmed not only by the unexpected visit but by what Jed had to say. Owen Black. She could hardly believe it. She remembered the day shortly after she and Gabe had moved south, when they went to see Owen to have their wills drawn. Being an "eyes" person, Mattie had seen something in Owen Black's eyes she didn't like, but when she mentioned it later to Gabe, he felt certain Owen was reputable.

"But Lovey," he'd said, trying to reassure her, especially since the wills had already been taken care of, "he came recommended." After seeing her face, however, he'd told her, "Look, I don't want you feeling the least bit uncomfortable. Let's wait a while, and then we'll find us another lawyer."

Of course, they got busy with plans for furnishing the condominium and making new friends. And Gabe loved his golf. So, "finding another lawyer" slid lower on their to-do list.

Sadly, it wasn't long before Mattie got word that Gabe had suffered a fatal heart attack while playing golf, and her world was shattered.

She gave a long sigh, and then found herself thinking about Eva. She tried to imagine Eva and her cruise plans, and how she would've looked and acted on board a cruise ship. It reminded her of an earlier incident. Shortly before Mattie and Gabe moved south, they were making up a picnic lunch and planning an outing over at the beach by Cedar Point and invited Eva to go. Surprisingly, she joined them.

But Mattie would never forget the bathing suit Eva wore that day: a loud, blindingly bright orange "thing," scattered with patches of sequins and glitter.

"Are you trying to light up the world or was that all they had left at Bargain Town?" Mattie had asked.

"I think this swimsuit is very attractive," Eva answered with a self-righteous smile. "After all, people have been staring at me ever since we got here."

"I can imagine."

Today Mattie replayed over and over in her mind Jed's news about Eva and Owen Black. What did he see in her? Mattie wondered. It wasn't that Eva was unattractive,

Mattie thought, and she had a fairly nice figure; it's just that her lights were running on dim, and she behaved like a spoiled brat. More to the point, what did Eva see in him? Short and pudgy, he waddled when he walked and had the personality of a turnip.

In a way, though, Mattie could see how Owen, given the right circumstances, might have been attracted to Eva, especially when she'd thrown herself at him, according to the secretary, and with him being newly divorced. Of course, he probably hadn't been treated to one of her "high-octane" temper tantrums, yet. Just wait, Owen, Mattie thought; just you wait.

Actually, the full impact of Jed's news was just beginning to sink in. But Mattie couldn't possibly have imagined what Eva and Owen Black had really been up to.

"Mrs. Morgan?" It was Lauren who poked her head in the doorway. "I wanted to let you know. That lecture on the plants and stuff is tomorrow at two. Think y'all can make it?"

"Tomorrow at two? I'll be there." Mattie thanked Lauren for coming by, and then slipped into her tennies. "Think I'll go for a walk. Better than sitting around here."

On her way out, Mattie checked again at the tiny mailroom and to her delight, this time Harry the mail clerk was there, sorting, and stacking things with rhythmic efficiency.

She tried to explain casually to him what she needed, not wanting to give away any of her plans for the flyers. "Any chance of getting a few sheets of plain paper and some coloring markers, Harry?"

Harry balked, momentarily stopping his sorting. "Oh, we can't be giving things away, just like that, Miss Mattie. You need a special order! Gotta' keep things orderly." He sort of sang out the word "orderly." Mattie watched him return to his sorting and resorting of envelopes and papers, almost in a trance, while he spoke. "Yup, gotta' keep things or-der-ly."

"Please, Harry. I really need them."

"But what in the world d'y'all want with paper and coloring pens, Miss Mattie?" he asked, all the while sorting and re-sorting, shuffling and re-shuffling as he spoke. Her head followed the action, back and forth, like someone watching a ping-pong game. She blew a puff of air into that springy curl that hung over one eye.

When he asked again what she wanted the supplies for, Mattie lost it. "We want to make you our poster child!" she blurted out. Harry continued on, unruffled. It wasn't going to be easy to make her point with him in that shuffling-and-sorting mode and making all those moves like a robot. She had to think of something, fast.

Suddenly, she began in an overly dramatic voice, "Harry, you don't understand. They're for my, my children!" She looked straight at him. Her brow rose above her pleading eyes, one hand at her chest. "The children are living with a friend," she said, giving a little sniff, "and she can't afford to buy things like—sniff—paper and markers for my dear little ones." Another sniff. "Won't you help them, pleeeze?" Eyes sincere, almost begging, near tears.

It worked. As if by magic, Harry's sorting and shuffling came to an abrupt halt. He gazed at her, and then sounded almost apologetic. "I never would've known that y'all had little ones, Miss Mattie."

"Most people don't," she said, trying to keep a straight face and look pathetic at the same time.

Harry lowered his voice. "Now don't y'all go getting upset like that. We'll take care of them young 'uns, don't you worry," and he handed over some plain paper and markers. Then he whispered, "But don't y'all be tellin' nobody 'bout this, hear?"

Though she appeared on the verge of tears, Mattie solemnly nodded and thanked him.

"And my children thank you, too, Harry."

"Well, I hope them young 'uns have a good time coloring," he said, smiling with pride at his good deed.

"Oh, we will...er...they will!" she answered brightly, suddenly back to normal. "Thanks, Harry!" And she scooted off.

Chuckling to herself, Mattie carried the supplies to her room and began working at her little table on sample flyers.

She noticed Clare in the hall and called to her. "I could use some help," she said. As Clare came into the room, Mattie lowered her voice. "I've got the stuff we need for the flyers. Close the door."

"How'd you get all this?" Clare asked, sitting down next to Mattie at the table. "Oh, Hyper Harry must've been there today."

Mattie grinned. "He's my accomplice." She showed Clare a sample of one of the colorful flyers she'd been working on that read:

> "BORED? TIRED OF BEING TREATED LIKE DIRT? JOIN THE RALLY AT MATTIE'S AT 2:00 ON THE 23rd AND START LIVING AGAIN.
> IF YOU DON'T GET INVOLVED, YOU'RE PART OF THE PROBLEM!"

A look of skepticism suddenly crossed Clare's face. "Mattie, I don't know. I mean, what are we getting ourselves into?" she asked, sagging.

Mattie could sense her friend was getting cold feet and asked pointedly, "Are you choosing to be part of the problem?" Their eyes met. Clare looked away, and then gradually a smile crept across her face. She nodded toward the flyer and said, "You might want to add something about our rights."

"Ooh, that's great, Clare! Good thinking."

The women worked for a while, making up a bunch of flyers. Finally, Mattie said, "I think that's enough for now, don't you?"

Clare nodded and they agreed to meet at midnight to distribute their works of art. They both giggled, just talking about it. "Our midnight dirty work," Clare dubbed it.

"Bring a flashlight," Mattie reminded her.

At midnight, when they showed up in the darkened hallway, Clare shone her flashlight on Mattie, who was wearing red and black pajamas. She had the flyers tucked under one arm.

Mattie directed her flashlight on her pal, then let out a subdued, "Yikes!" and leaned closer. "Is that really you, Clare?" she whispered. Clare had spread a black, muddy concoction over her face, with openings for her eyes, nose and mouth, and she had on a wild jungle-print muumuu. "You look like you belong in a zoo!" Mattie whispered. "What's all that goop on your face?!"

"Night cream. Keeps wrinkles away."

"I'd be more worried about keeping the dogcatcher away," Mattie said, while Clare let out a subdued growl. Both of them fought to hold back snickers.

"Here's what we'll do," Mattie whispered, leading the way down the hall. "Just watch me." She approached one of the resident's rooms, directed the light toward the bottom of the door, and slipped one of the flyers underneath.

"There. They'll find it when they get up tomorrow morning." With a shrug, she said, "See? Nothing to it."

Clare took a handful of the flyers, and they continued on until all of them had been distributed.

"Good job!" they whispered in unison, exchanging high fives.

"Now let's get back before someone sees us," Mattie said.

Just then, they heard a sound from behind. They both whirled around, as Mattie caught the beam from another flashlight. Shielding her eyes with one hand, she asked cautiously,

"What is it? Who's there?!"

"Looking for me, Passion Pie?"

Mattie recognized the nasal voice. "Bernard," she groaned, with one hand over her heart. "You scared the daylights out of me! Turn that blasted light off, you weasel!"

He doused the light but moved closer to the women. "They all play hard to get," he muttered, chuckling in the darkness. "Wanna' try one of my smooches on for size?"

Mattie heard him approaching, making silly kissing sounds. She gave Clare a nudge.

"Growl, Clare, growl!" Then she aimed her flashlight at Clare and lit up her frightening, mud-packed face, while Clare did a convincing monster impression, raising her hands, curling her fingers and making a subdued growling noise. Then Mattie switched her light to Bernard.

On seeing Clare's spooky get-up, a trembling, bug-eyed Bernard inhaled several quick breaths, dropped his flashlight, and hightailed it out of there. Mattie and Clare went into a fit of giggling and couldn't stop.

Suddenly, Clare clutched her stomach and began to groan. "Oh...oh, no..."

"What is it, Clare?" Mattie asked. "What's wrong?"

"I...have...to pee!" she blurted. Mattie let out a snort of laughter and tried to help her pal along. "I can't walk with my legs crossed!" Clare protested, somewhere between agony and hysterics.

Doing their best to keep from disturbing any of the residents, Mattie and Clare made it back to their hall, stifling their giggles. When they approached Mattie's room, she said, "Come on in, Clare. You can use my bathroom."

"Sorry, Mattie," Clare said, barely able to speak. "It's too late."

All that night, Mattie couldn't sleep. Visions of her flyers and the "midnight dirty work" scrambled her mind. At no time had she thought she'd done anything wrong. It was more an obligation. The folks at Autumn Leaves needed someone to lead them, to "get them going," as Lillian had put it the other day. Well, Mattie was good at getting results and she knew it. So that took care of that.

She fell in and out of a restless sleep, one time waking to the thought of being with Clare earlier, giggling all over again, then thinking of Bernard and what a strange little man he was. In the distance, she could hear the katydids through her open window. Their chirping lulled her into a sound sleep.

The sun was just peeking around the edges of her curtains, when suddenly Mattie sat straight up in her bed. She remembered putting one of the flyers underneath the door to Fae's room. Of course, being bedridden with the stroke, Fae wouldn't have been able to retrieve it. But that meant her flyer would still be lying on the floor! What if Fae's "now and then" therapist just happened by today, of all days, and found the flyer?!

"Yikes!" she cried, jumping out of bed. After hastily changing into her sweats and tennies, she headed down the hall toward Fae's room. When she got there, she noticed the door was open. "Uh, oh," she murmured. "Oh, please let the flyer still be on the floor."

Peeking inside, Mattie's worst fears were realized. An aide stood at Fae's bed trying to work with her. Seeing the woman, Mattie sagged. She stood back, unseen, while the aide spoke in a loud, demeaning voice to Fae, who was being totally uncooperative.

"Y'all will have to go back to the hospital, if you don't start helping y'self!" the aide spouted. "We can't be wasting our time here, 'less y'all do your part."

Mattie cringed. Something in the woman's demeanor reminded her of how a female General Patton might have sounded.

Using the moment, Mattie quietly stepped into the room, her eyes searching the floor for the flyer. Then she spotted it, less than an inch from Patton's foot. The flyer apparently had been swept up when the door was opened. Mattie strolled over to the bed, gave the flyer a brush with her shoe, sliding it under the bed and out of sight, and at the same time, asked, "How's Fae getting along?"

Patton wheeled around and glared suspiciously at Mattie. "Where'd you come from? And what are you doing here?" she demanded.

Mattie shrugged. "I'm just a friend of hers," she said innocently. "I wondered how she was doing, that's all."

"She won't help h'self," the aide said crisply, throwing her hands up in defeat. "It's been weeks and she's not gettin' any stronger." Shaking her head and grumbling, Ms. Patton huffed and puffed out of the room in frustration.

Mattie made a face at her behind her back. Once she was out of sight, Mattie stretched her foot under Fae's bed to bring the flyer back her way, grateful the aide hadn't spotted it.

With the flyer safely in hand, she turned to Fae. Leaning over the bed, Mattie took hold of Fae's hand and gave it a gentle squeeze. She was astonished when Fae returned the gesture with a very strong grip!

"Why, you rascal," Mattie said, pretending to scold her. "Holding out on the therapist, are you?" Then she stood up straight. "I think you might need another visit from that puppy."

Mary A. Berger

4

The sound of waves splashing gently against the white sand of Condado Beach at San Juan lulled Eva into a dreamy mood of self-satisfaction. After taking another swallow of Chardonnay delivered by the good-looking, dark-skinned beach waiter, she sighed a deep sigh of relief. The sun streaming down, the gentle breeze of the Caribbean—everything was perfect, now.

Glancing around, she noticed nearly all the colorful beach chairs and chaises that lined the beach were in use, the area was that popular. Then the sounds of other beach-goers, laughing and mingling together, caught her attention.

One couple in particular stood out. The woman, probably in her early thirties with blond hair and a model's face and figure, seemed to glide across the sand as she walked; her partner, a good-looking, late thirties man, strolled alongside carrying a drink in each hand. The woman wore a one-piece, all white swimsuit and, Eva noted, just enough jewelry to be considered fashionably understated, as she'd heard the term used.

They seemed to be searching for a place to land. Suddenly, Eva sucked in a deep breath. The two of them were coming towards her.

"Oh, Jason, here's an empty chaise," the woman said, pointing to one that happened to adjoin a small beach table next to Eva. "This will be fine." She turned to Eva. "Unless it's taken?"

Embarrassed by her own gawking, Eva tried to regain her composure. "Uh, n-no, it's okay. You can use it." And she gave a silly laugh.

If the woman noticed Eva's awkwardness, she didn't show it. She smiled, took one of the drinks from "Jason," and thanked him. What little jewelry the woman wore was gorgeous,

Eva noticed. She didn't want to stare but it was hard not to. Heart-shaped diamond earrings, a turquoise studded thumb ring with a matching toe ring. But the thick shiny bracelet sprinkled with diamonds was what caught Eva's eye. She'd never seen a piece of jewelry so stunning; probably platinum, she assumed.

"Mmm, the Margaritas are extra delicious today," the woman said pleasantly, lying back and adjusting her sunglasses.

Eva was still staring, but caught herself and replied, "Uh, yes, so's the Chardonnay." At a loss as to what else to say to someone like her, Eva chugged a couple more swallows of her wine. Then it dawned on her that the woman's friend was standing off to one side, so, nodding at the man, she asked, "What about him?" "I'll let him use my chaise so you two can be together. I assume he's your husband, or?" Eva started to move from her seat.

"No, no; stay put," said the woman. Then with a little laugh, she added, "And no, dear, he's not my husband. He's my bodyguard."

Eva could barely contain herself. "Oh-h-h . . . oh, I see," she said, even more mesmerized.

The woman sat back and took another sip of her drink. They sat silently for a while, and then finally she asked Eva, "Are you new here?"

"Uh, no...well, I come now and then," Eva stammered.

"I don't think I've seen you before," the woman said. They exchanged a bit of small talk, mostly about the weather and the gorgeous setting. Some time passed, then after downing the last of her Margarita, the woman surprised Eva when she said, "By the way, I'm Christine."

She extended her hand to Eva, who returned the handshake and introduced herself. "It's nice to meet you, Eva," Christine said graciously. Then with a glance toward the bodyguard, she said, "Well, we have to be leaving." She turned to Eva. "The limo's picking us up to run out to the club. Maybe I'll see you another day."

Eva was almost speechless. "Okay," she finally said, giving another silly laugh. "I'll probably be back tomorrow. This beach is too nice to stay away from."

"I agree! See you around, Eva." As Christine and Jason left, they ran into a classy looking older couple whom they apparently knew and went off with them.

Eva watched, her tongue almost hanging out with envy. She lay back on the chaise, puffed with self-importance. To think that she was here at this lovely, world-class resort, mingling with someone like Christine; it was almost too much for her to take in. She finished her wine, and snapped her fingers at the waiter to bring another glass.

The next day, Eva was where she said she'd be, at the beach. Luckily, she had bought two new bathing suits, one a bright crimson with chartreuse polka dots; the other a more subdued brown and grey stripe, which she wore that day. And of course, she still had the snazzy bright orange one sprinkled with sequins she'd worn to Cedar Point with her father and Hattie.

Trying not to be too obvious, she searched the beach for Christine but didn't see her or the bodyguard. She imagined they'd probably hopped a jet down to Rio! This time, Eva ordered a Margarita, just to be like Christine. Between the warm sunshine and the drink, she began feeling drowsy, and soon nodded off.

She started to dream:

She saw her father and Mattie dancing closely at their wedding, and she, herself, was there with Jason, flaunting him as her bodyguard. Everyone in the dream was quite impressed and flocked around the two of them, completely ignoring Gabe and Mattie...

"Eva . . . Eva . . ." It was Christine. "You must've partied all night last night!" she said with a laugh.

In her mild stupor, Eva frowned at Christine and said dumbly, "Huh? What'd you say?" Horrified then at sounding so ridiculous in front of Christine, she began apologizing.

Christine was gracious and brushed her off. "Don't worry, dear. This place can do things like that to a person." Jason had toted a beach chair over for her to use, while he flopped down a few feet away on a towel.

"Eva," Christine said after a while, "may I ask a question? How come an attractive woman like you is here alone?"

Eva's smile began to evaporate. "What do you mean?" she asked hastily, but soon caught herself, especially at being called "attractive" by Christine.

"Oh, I'm sorry," Christine said. "I didn't mean to imply anything. It's just that, well, it's not often I see someone here by themselves."

Eva gave a shaky answer. "Oh, we...uh...broke up. He was...um...running around and I just wanted to...to get away." She stared off in the distance, forced a sad expression, and hoped Christine hadn't picked up on her phony story.

Christine sounded totally sympathetic. "You poor dear. That can tear a person up. I know; I've been there."

Eva couldn't imagine any guy in his right mind breaking up with someone like her, but she was glad Christine seemed to buy her story.

They sat quietly for a moment, and then Christine called over to Jason and asked him to get her another Margarita. "And bring one for my friend," she added, smiling and patting Eva's hand.

"Oh, well, thanks!" Eva exclaimed, absolutely enthralled. Again, she felt drawn to that bracelet Christine was wearing. She nearly drooled, watching it reflect the sun's rays each time Christine moved her arm. Simply beautiful.

"Eva," Christine said, "you've probably traveled to The Bahamas, haven't you?" Eva nodded dumbly. "There's a great beach club there called Casa del Sol. Ever been?"

"Why...uh...sure. I mean, I think so. Let's see ...Casa Del Sol." She seemed to be digging for the name. Finally, she waved her hand and blurted, "I've been so many places it's hard for me to remember them all."

"Oh, me, too!" Christine appeared to be warming up to Eva, even though Eva had never heard of the Bahamas place, let alone having visited there.

"And what about the Galapagos!" Christine was on a roll then. "Aren't they fabulous? And Greece!" She let out an audible sigh. "But, you know, I've never seen

Antarctica!" she said with a laugh. "And I've always wanted to go; don't ask me why! Maybe this season I'll do it."

She lowered her voice and added, "If my investments pay off!" Somehow, Eva was certain they would.

Jason brought their Margaritas and returned to his spot on the beach towel, working on a cold beer.

Eva couldn't believe her luck. Here she was, in this beautiful place, chatting with Christine, with a bodyguard on the side, of all things! It was starting to go to her head.

After a while, the older, nice-looking couple whom Christine had left with the day before showed up. They smiled at Eva, and then asked how "our beautiful lady" was doing today. Christine laughed amiably, and then introduced them to Eva. "Sybil and Milford, this is a new friend of mine, Eva."

The outfit Sybil was wearing, a white cover-up over a navy swimsuit, complimented her lovely tanned face and silver hair. "So nice to meet you, Eva," she said, taking Eva's hand, while Milford stood back smiling and nodding politely to Eva. Sybil then turned to Christine. "But we really must keep moving. Dinner plans with Tracy and Bill tonight on their yacht."

"They invited us, too," Christine said, with a hint of regret. "But, we're heading up the beach. Some friends are doing a luau. Have a wonderful time with Tracy and Bill!"

After they'd left, Christine settled back and took some more of her drink. A little later, Jason checked his watch and said something to her.

"Oh, is it that time already?" asked Christine. She gathered herself, and then the two of them started to leave. "So nice chatting with you again, Eva," she said, smiling. "Maybe we'll see you another time."

I'm sure you will, Eva wanted to say, but she only nodded, and remembered at the last minute to thank Christine again for the drink.

Alone on her chaise, Eva felt overcome with satisfaction. She couldn't quite grasp her good fortune in meeting Christine and her friends. If she played her cards right, she'd be part of that circle before long. But she didn't want to appear too eager.

"One step at a time," she murmured, and only the swaying palms and the warm Caribbean breeze heard her.

Mary A. Berger

 5

The spring rains were doing their thing again. Back in her room, Mattie watched the sky grow darker by the minute. With the downpour, she figured there wasn't much point in calling Scooter's owner and asking her to bring the dog out in the rain.

Heaving a long sigh, she set her book down and decided to do a little dusting to kill time. That took all of ten minutes. She'd talked to Clare, who said she was pooped from all their gallivanting in the halls the night before and was going to "try to recover" with a nap. Not only that, she was dying to know what Jed Mitchell had learned about Eva and her boyfriend, if anything. She still found it hard to believe the story about her own stepdaughter and her own lawyer having a fling somewhere in the Caribbean. She could imagine the natives whispering about the *loco* couple.

After a light lunch of chicken noodle soup and crackers, Mattie read some more and worked a crossword puzzle in the newspaper. In a rare moment, except for when she watched the news or a Braves baseball game, Mattie turned on her television and got a game show. "Cheddar Champs" was one bunch of crazies in wet suits diving into a vat of cheese, digging for money at the bottom.

Mattie chuckled and shook her head, then went back to her book.

When two o'clock rolled around, Mattie attended the gardening lecture, if only to please Lauren. It simply took place in the front lobby, where someone had set up five or six folding chairs in a semicircle. Two other people, a man named Clint whom she'd met earlier, and a woman whose name Mattie didn't know, came along and took their seats. Clint slouched back into his chair, feet stretched out in front of him, hands folded across his middle, as though settling in for a nice nap.

A man arrived and introduced himself to the crowd of three as Melvin Kerr. "Thank you all for coming and I'll get right down to business. Our topic today is "Transforming Common Weeds into Classic Keepers."

Mattie slumped. A lecture on weeds?

Melvin opened his talk with a little blurb about his gardening expertise, even referring to some of his weeds as his "precious little lovelies." That got him off on the wrong foot right away, as far as Mattie was concerned. He sounded silly, like a dirty old man bragging about his collection of girlfriends.

But Mattie wanted to be fair and give the man a chance. He went on to explain about the various types of weeds, which grew locally, and about how easily they could be identified, even along the highway. As if folks at a housing center couldn't wait to get out to the nearest highway to find their favorite weed! Mattie thought with a smirk.

"...and my friend, chickweed, is another favorite. To find this marvelous specimen..." He droned on like the sound of a distant lawn mower.

After a while, Mattie decided the lecture was as lively as watching a tree grow. She was soon lulled into a nap, giving a hearty snore with each breath. Suddenly she bolted upright when Clint gave a loud yawn that could have been heard in the next county. Clint and the woman laughed. Even stuffy Melvin Kerr couldn't keep a straight face.

He came over to Mattie but she shooed him away.

"Hell's bells!" she wailed. "How do you expect anyone to sit through five minutes of this stuff?! All that nonsense about your weeds and your 'precious lovelies'. Give me a break!" She jumped out of her chair and told him pointedly, "You've been wanderin' in the woods too long, Weed Boy!"

Melvin Kerr grew indignant, gathered up his "precious little lovelies" and left in a huff.

As Mattie walked away grumbling to herself, she heard Clint and the woman applauding and calling out, "Way to go, Mattie! You tell 'em!"

Leaving the lobby, Mattie was surprised to see Mr. Bates walking towards her. "Mrs. Morgan, I don't know what to say," he began apologizing. "I heard everything from my office, and this was absolutely the worst excuse for a *program* that I've ever seen." Mattie stood in amazement, especially when he confessed, "I fell asleep, too."

They chatted for a moment, and she let Mr. Bates know how disappointed she was. But she ended up feeling a little sorry for him. After all, he'd had nothing to do with the scheduling, he told her. "We'll try harder to offer something that's more interesting," he said. Yet both he and Mattie knew those were just words and nothing more.

"Hello, Jean? It's Mattie." Mattie was calling Scooter's owner to see if today would be good for her to bring the dog over to the center. "Oh, I'm doing fine, thanks. I was wondering if—" Mattie stopped in mid-sentence, then smiled and nodded. "Oh, good. That would be great! All right, then; we'll meet you out back in about an hour. Thank you!"

Mattie was tickled as much about seeing the dog as she was talking to an "outsider." Too excited to do anything else, not even glance at the newspaper, or rinse her breakfast dishes, she took off for Clare's and ran into her in the hall.

"Clare, guess what?"

"Our own private chef is coming to prepare dinner for us!" said Clare, wide-eyed.

Shaking her head, Mattie told her, "You're weird." Then she lowered her voice. "Jean's bringing the puppy over again. Let's go outside and wait for her." On the way to the back porch, Mattie clued Clare in on her visit with Fae the other day.

"She actually squeezed your hand hard?" Clare asked, almost in disbelief. "There's a rumor going around that she's getting worse. I don't get it."

"I think it's her so-called therapist," Mattie scoffed. "What a holy terror that woman is. I hope I never need her for therapy; that would be like working with Godzilla!"

Outdoors they chatted a while before meeting up with Scooter and his owner. "Thank you so much, Jean," Mattie said, as the woman arrived and handed over the dog. "Don't worry; we'll take good care of him."

"I know, Mattie," Jean replied with her good-natured drawl. "I'm not worried, y'all. I do need to have him back later this afternoon, though. He's on his way to a training center up in Asheville. It's where they teach dogs to work with the handicapped."

Clare frowned. "Isn't he a little young?"

Jean shook her head. "No, they start early and you'd be amazed how well they do." She smiled, while petting Scooter good-bye. "Actually, y'all gave me the idea to get him into the program when you borrowed him a few weeks ago for that lady with the stroke."

Mattie smiled in appreciation. They thanked Jean again and headed back inside with Scooter tucked beneath Mattie's jacket, as before.

Approaching Fae's area, Mattie noticed Gwen peeking around a corner, then pulling back when she saw them. She nudged Clare. "Did you catch that?" She nodded in the direction where she'd seen Gwen.

"What was it?"

"Gwen," Mattie whispered. "It's almost like she's watching us."

Clare gave a snort and did a little boogie dance. "Think she saw that?"

"What is the deal with that woman?" asked Mattie.

"Aw, Mattie, where's the love?" Clare teased, and they shrugged if off.

When they reached Fae's room, Clare stepped inside, and then gave an "all clear" signal. "It's okay, Mattie; come on in."

Leaning over the bed, Mattie set the puppy down and encouraged Fae to pet him by placing Fae's hand on the dog and helping move her hand down his back. To their surprise, Fae began petting the dog on her own!

"That's the hand with the iron grip," Mattie told Clare. "She'll be up mopping her floor before long!" Clare chuckled, and both were happy to see Fae's progress.

Suddenly, Clare whispered, "Someone's coming."

"Yikes." Mattie snatched up Scooter, who seemed livelier today than before, and hastily tucked him under the covers.

Clare was already at the door. It was Lillian, and Clare returned with some notes from her for Mattie's rally. "Lillian wondered if I'd give you these the next time I saw you," said Clare. "So, here!" And she handed them to Mattie.

Mattie was elated. Grinning, she brought the fidgeting Scooter out of his hiding place and set him on the floor, while she glanced at the notes. She didn't notice the door, slightly ajar, open just wide enough to let a puppy through. Scooter took off.

The women both sucked in a gasp. Mattie crammed the notes in her pocket and they flew after the dog. He had already disappeared around a corner. "How'd he get away so fast?!" squealed Clare.

They searched all the empty rooms, the lobby, the broom closet, even around the medics' station, a modest little stand with some drawers, but there was no sign of Scooter. Frantic, Mattie said, "We didn't check the rest rooms. He might've slipped in when someone opened the door!"

They peeked into the ladies' room but found no trace of Scooter. At the door to the men's room, they paused; stood face to face, and then with a shrug, Mattie opened the door a crack.

In a deep-throated, manly voice, she called out, "Anyone in here?"

Clare chuckled to herself.

"I think it's clear," Mattie said, and they tiptoed in.

"There he is!" spouted Clare. "By the sink!" They both made a lunge for the dog. He darted into a nearby stall, flopped onto the floor, rump in the air, tail wagging, and watched them.

"Little monster!" said Clare, gritting her teeth.

Mattie was already down on her hands and knees and snatched him up.

At that moment, the door to the stall swung open. It was Mr. Reemes.

He jumped back startled. "What's going on here?" he demanded. When he saw who it was, he calmed down and crossed his arms. "Well, well. If it isn't Mrs. Morgan and Mrs. Tibbitts," he said, in a demeaning tone. "Tell me, was the ladies room too crowded?" He stepped aside. "Into the hall, ladies and dog, if you don't mind," he directed them sharply.

Before he could say another word, Mattie handed Scooter over to Clare. "Here, Clare, why don't you take him back to Jean?" Clare agreed, and then headed for the back door, leaving Mattie with Mr. Reemes.

"Mrs. Morgan," he said, "I'd like you to step into my office." He stretched an arm outward, directing her to his "office," which wasn't much more than the size of a walk-in closet.

"Mrs. Morgan, I thought we had discussed our rules here," he said, hovering over her. "Didn't I explain that you have to follow them?"

"Yes, but—"

"No buts about it. Rules are rules. And we don't allow animals here at Autumn Leaves." And he attempted to escort her out, as though she were a ten-year-old. But Mattie wasn't about to be brushed off. "We're not children," she said, refusing to budge. "When are you going to wake up and join the rest of the world?"

"Please leave, now." Mr. Reemes sat down at his desk and repeated, "Now!"

Instead, Mattie plunked into a chair opposite his desk, leaned forward and glared at him, her sweet blue eyes turning to bolts of blue lightning. "Maybe you haven't heard how therapeutic a dog can be for someone who's ill, like Fae Munn!" she let him know. "Dogs are brought into places like this all the time, sir."

Mr. Reemes had turned red up to his ears, and his glazed eyes told her he was about to explode. But Mattie continued, leaning closer and getting in his face. "Look," she said slowly, emphasizing each word, "we've got someone here who's had a stroke, and she's responding to that dog!" Then she added, "Do the math!"

At that moment, the sound of someone stepping into the office stopped Mattie's rant. "Everything okay here, Mrs. Morgan? Jim?" It was Mr. Bates.

"Yes," Mattie said smugly, rising from her chair. "I was just leaving." Mr. Bates watched as she passed in front of him with her head held proudly. Out in the hall, she heard the office door close behind her. "Whew," she muttered.

Inside Jim Reemes' office, Harold Bates tried to soften the encounter with Mattie.

"That woman is poison," Reemes growled. "I don't know what we're going to do about her."

"Wait a minute, Jim." Mr. Bates shoved a newspaper article under his nose. "Better take a look at this before you say anything more."

"What is it?"

"An article that was published in the local paper and in several newspapers across this area. It's actually good PR for Autumn Leaves."

Mr. Reemes muttered parts of the article aloud. "'...local housing center...dog helps stroke victim...start of new trend...'" Mr. Reemes squinted his eyes and said, "So today wasn't the first time she's brought the dog in." Rubbing his chin he added, "I wonder what else she's been doing behind our backs. She's obviously responsible for this!" he said, slapping the article with the back of his hand.

"Calm down, Jim. And, no, she didn't have anything to do with that article. But I know who did."

"Who, then?"

"The dog's owner." Mr. Bates went on to explain that he'd seen her up the road near her farm with the dog one day and stopped to talk to her. "This publicity could give us a big boost," he went on to say. "It has a nice touch. Besides, the newspaper called my office. They might want to do a follow-up."

Jim Reemes' eyebrows were on the ceiling, as he peered over his glasses at Mr. Bates. "Oh?" Swallowing hard, he caught himself. Half-heartedly, he agreed about the public relations aspect, and thanked Harold Bates for bringing the article to his attention.

After Mr. Bates left, Reemes crumpled the article and tossed it in the wastebasket. Staring into space, he murmured, "This isn't good. Think I'll get a hold of Wynn."

Leaving his office, he pulled out a set of keys, and went over and unlocked the room where earlier Mattie had thought they kept the troublemakers locked up.

Back in her room, Mattie sat quietly in her chair. She not only felt proud of how she'd handled the encounter with Mr. Reemes, but also felt even more strongly that it was long overdue.

The circumstances just hadn't been right, until today. How could anyone in his or her right mind be so concerned about a puppy visiting the center? You'd think he'd want what was best for the needier people there. She gave a little sniff. Unless he truly doesn't want what's best for them. But why? Things just didn't add up.

She thought long and hard about the situation. It was becoming more obvious to Mattie that Reemes was trying to hide something, or simply trying to keep everyone under his thumb. That thought, too, became clearer every day, and a little more frightening. She wondered what his position really was, and what part the owner, Wynn Prescott, played in things. She was determined to find out, one way or another.

She decided to go see Clare and make sure Scooter, the little rascal, got back to his owner. Clare came to the door, holding an orange drink.

"Hey, Matts; c'mon in. I've got some news for you."

"What about the dog? Did he get back to Jean okay?"

"Oh, that little monkey. He nearly got away from me again before I got outside! Yes, he's back home again." Clare was about to set her drink down. Then, turning to Mattie, she asked, "Want some?"

"Oh, yes. I'd love some orange juice." Right now, the juice sounded especially good to Mattie, and she was anxious to share the story of her encounter with Mr. Reemes.

Clare snickered. "Okay, but it's not entirely orange juice," she cautioned.

"Doesn't matter; I'll take some."

Clare filled a glass part way and handed it to her. They raised their glasses in a toast, and Clare said, "Mattie, I hated leaving you all alone with that shark, Reemes, but you were right; we had to get the dog back. So tell me, what happened?" She took a long swallow of her drink, while Mattie told her the story.

Clare was all ears. "Told him good, didn't you? You go, girl!" she said, swallowing more of her drink.

"Mr. Bates finally came in and broke things up," Mattie said, "but I left there proud of myself." She looked at the drink she was sipping. "Say, this is pretty good. Best orange juice I ever had, in fact."

"I know," Clare said, grinning. "And this is my third one." By then, she wasn't thinking quite as clearly as usual and her words came out a little skewed. "Actually, there's a name for this drink. It's called a . . ." She looked a little befuddled. ". . . a Harvey Wallhanger...er...Barvey Halldanger...Harvey Ballwanger."

The two of them burst out laughing, and Mattie had to set her drink down before spilling it. Unused to drinking anything other than a little wine now and then, Mattie was starting to notice the effects of the Harvey Wallbanger.

"Y'know, Clare," she said; "it feels as if I'm actually making a little progress with Mr. Reemes. Maybe after a few more of these run-ins with him, he'll turn into a human being."

Clare gave a snort. "Don't count your . . . kitchens." She frowned and tried again. "Don't kiss your chickens . . . "

Again, Mattie chuckled. "Are you trying to say, 'Don't count your chickens before they're hatched', Clare?"

"Yeah," Clare said brightly. "That's it."

Mattie had to pat her eyes with a tissue from giggling. Then she grew serious. "But what's this news you have, Clare?"

Clare chuckled, and then paused, trying to remember what it was she was going to tell Mattie. "Oh, I'm leaving tomorrow. Going up to my daughter's for a week."

"How nice. And where is she?"

"Up in Ohio. Gahanna, by Columbus." She frowned comically. "Or is it Columbus, by Gahanna?" They laughed again. Then Clare got serious and let out a sigh. "Anyway, I hope I'm doing the right thing. The last time I was there her kids drove me crazy. But they're older now, so things should be easier."

"As long as you're back for my rally. Don't forget, it's next Thursday." Mattie popped up out of the chair and said, "I've got a few things to do and some stuff to check on, so I'm out of here. Thanks for the 'orange juice', Clare," she said grinning. Leaning over, she gave her friend a hug. "In case I don't see you before you leave."

Returning the hug, Clare said, "Okay, and don't worry, I'll be back by Thursday. Then she added with a smirk, "Maybe sooner." She looked a little skeptical. "I wish you could come with me, Mattie."

"Oh, thanks; but you need to get away from here for a while. Just go and have a good time."

6

The following day was sunny with a spectacular sky overhead. A perfect day for

Mattie to get her walk in. In the distance, she could hear the sounds of a tractor and assumed it was from Jean's farm.

She was itching to get back out to the greenhouse. Donning a pair of blue jeans and a work shirt, she brought along her gloves and an old trowel, saved from previous gardening projects "in my other life" she thought with a smirk. Then she checked for her whistle and stuffed a few tissues in her pocket.

Along the way back to the greenhouse, she paused at an old shed that had previously been vacated. Today a heavyset man wearing overalls was there and popped his head out from behind a mower he was working on. He looked surprised to see Mattie but spoke to her easily.

"Mornin', ma'am. Doin' okay?"

"Oh, yes," Mattie said. "I'm good."

"Y'all live here?"

"Yup."

"Well, I'm Hank. I do the yard work around here."

Mattie gave a snort. "Then you must not be very busy, Hank, because there's not much in the way of yard to take care of."

Hank chuckled. "Yes, ma'am. But I do what I can. This mower's older than dirt. Who knows, maybe by the time I get it running, there'll be some grass to mow!"

Mattie introduced herself and they continued their conversation. "You seem to know your way around," Hank said, after she told him where she was headed. He removed his Braves baseball cap and ran a hand over his balding head. "Can't say as I ever seen no greenhouse, though," he said, replacing the cap. "But I've heard that this whole area used to be a nursery or 'tobaccy' farm or something."

"Is that right?"

He chuckled and said, "'Course, today most of them 'tobaccy' farms are down the tubes, just like the white lightnin's on its way out. Most folks have to get it from a 'special store' nowadays. Where's the fun in that?"

She laughed appreciatively. Then he got a big grin on his face and started in with a routine of often-used one-liners. "By the way, Miss Mattie: y'know, I just had skylights put in my apartment. The people above me are furious." She chuckled again, so he added another. "My wife told me she'd like to get away and go some place she hasn't been in a long time. I suggested the kitchen."

Mattie laughed harder. "How do you come up with these things?"

"Just my nature," he told her. "I love to make people laugh."

She wondered where this guy had been keeping himself; his humor was truly uplifting. "Well, it was nice to meet you, Hank. I'm sure I'll see you around."

"Yes, ma'am."

Mattie continued on her way. As she approached the greenhouse, the sun disappeared behind a dark cloud. She knew that in these mountains a storm could brew and the weather could change in a flash, even though the skies might be clear at the moment.

Mattie got right to work. After a while, she could actually see some progress. Piling together some rubble and chunks of glass, she felt a few sprinkles. By now, the storm clouds were building. Mattie knew she'd better be getting back.

"Just one more piece," she muttered, snatching up a last large shard of glass and tossing it into the pile. A sudden stinging sensation in her hand made her gasp in pain. "Damn!" she muttered. Looking down, she saw a bloody patch that had already appeared through a worn spot on her glove.

She squeezed one of the tissues into her hand, snatched up her trowel, and started back, upset with herself at being so careless. By the time she got back, she was drenched with rain. Some of the residents were watching the storm from the back porch. Lauren had come outside to join them. When she caught sight of the waterlogged Mattie, she flew across the yard to her.

"Mrs. Morgan, you're soaking wet! Where have you been?" She noticed Mattie's hand was tucked inside her shirt, and then saw the bloodstained tissue. Frightened, she led Mattie to the porch and demanded, "What's this? What happened?" Some of the others had gathered out of curiosity.

"For crying out loud, it's nothing," Mattie wailed, trying to make light of the cut. "It's just a little cut. I'll put a Band Aid on it."

"A little cut, my foot," Lauren said. "Come on, we're going inside." Mattie drew back, but Lauren was firm. "I insist," she let Mattie know.

"What'd I tell you?" Mattie began spouting. "Didn't I say someone could get hurt out there? If they'd cleaned up that area, none of this would be happening.   But no, nobody listens to me!"

The residents were buzzing and heads were turning.

After stopping by the medics' stand, Lauren escorted Mattie back to her room, where she applied some antiseptic and a gauze pad to her hand. Then Lauren proceeded to lecture Mattie in a stern, but caring way. "I don't want you out there picking up any more glass," she instructed. "We don't want anything to happen to you."

"I don't see why you're making such a fuss over this" Mattie complained, while secretly enjoying the attention.

Lauren had made her a cup of tea, and then stood over her. "What am I going to do with you?" she asked, the start of a smile creeping over her face.

"You've done enough already," Mattie told her appreciatively.

Word of the incident spread through the center. Lauren reported it to Mr. Bates, who went to see Mattie right away. "Mrs. Morgan, what's this I hear about you having a little accident?" he asked, after pulling out one of the chairs at her table.

"It was nothing," she came back. "But that area out at the old greenhouse needs work," she told him, holding up her injured hand, as though to prove her point. She had his undivided attention.

After expressing his concern for her, he promised he'd stop back again next day to see how she was doing. Then he went right over to Jim Reemes' office and told him about Mattie's accident.

"That woman, again?!" Reemes shot back. "What's next? The National Guard dropping by?" Impatiently, he flopped back into his chair.

"She does have a bad cut, Jim. And we should've had that area back there cleared out a long time ago." He gave Reemes a dubious look. "We've had one notice already." It was obvious Harold Bates was growing impatient. "I'd just hate to think of us getting involved in a lawsuit," he said, in an attempt to sound worried, while seriously doubting his own words.

"Jeez, you think she'd go that far, Harold?"

"She might. And I pity anyone who tries to stop her," Mr. Bates added, for good measure.

"Maybe you're right." After a moment, he asked, "Know where we can find a good clean-up crew?"

"I'll take care of it," Harold Bates said. On the way out he gave a barely audible, "Yesss."

Lying back on her pillow that night, the throbbing in Mattie's hand kept her awake.

Reluctantly, she took one of the aspirins Lauren had set out for her. How she longed for Gabe—gently stroking her hair, or holding her hand—he'd always been so kind, so caring. It was beyond her how he and Eva could even be related. Sad to say, he'd once told Mattie he felt

Eva would stop at nothing to have her own way. "Just keep an eye on her," Gabe had cautioned Mattie. Keep an eye on his *own daughter*, she recalled his words with dismay.

Now, after Jed's last visit, she was certain Eva knew the whereabouts of Gabe's will and probably had a huge hand in the events following Gabe's death. The missing will. His important papers. Their safe had been virtually cleared out! Mattie gave a long sigh, as the aspirin began to have a calming effect. The whole idea of the will was to see that she had a secure future. Near tears, she "raised up" a prayer to help herself cope, and then drifted off to sleep.

Next morning, Mattie awoke to the sounds of men's voices outside her window. She rubbed her eyes and threw back the blanket.

"Ow-w-w!" she wailed. Gingerly holding her hand, she went to the window and peeked out. To her surprise, she saw a pickup truck going across the grounds. It was carrying tools and had a couple of workmen on board. Since the truck was going toward the back of the property, Mattie assumed it was heading for Hank's old maintenance shed.

She showered and went about her usual morning routine, holding off her exercises because of her hand, and decided to take a couple of vitamins, instead. Smiling, as she swallowed a Vitamin E capsule, she thought of how Gabe used to tease her about it, how he'd heard the vitamin supposedly enhanced your sex life. That struck her as comical now in her present situation. Had Clare been there, she would've joked, "Hey, there's always Bernard."

Mattie shuddered at the thought, and then picked up the morning paper. After a while, she tossed it aside as boredom set in. Then she heard a tap at her door, which she purposely left open most of the time in hopes that Lauren might stop by.

"Who's there?" she called from her chair.

"Harold Bates."

"Oh, come in," she told him, smiling, and noticing he had used his first name and dropped the "Mr." He stepped in and asked how her hand was.

She glanced down at her hand and quipped, "Well, it's still here."

He smiled and his eyes brightened. "I have some good news. All that glass around the greenhouse is being picked up and hauled away. We sent a crew out this morning."

"So that's what the truck was all about. I saw it go by earlier."

"Yes. Hopefully, things will be taken care of." He glanced at his watch. "I hope your hand feels better soon, Mrs. Morgan." She thanked him and he left.

Mattie had mixed feelings about the clean-up thing. It was too much of a coincidence. Oh, she was glad to hear they were getting rid of the broken glass. But she also was smart enough to realize that fear of a lawsuit was probably behind it.

At least there was some positive action, she told herself, and that was worth something

It was Thursday the twenty-third, moments before Mattie's protest rally was scheduled. After straightening her kitchen and plumping the cushions on her recliner, she glanced around. She had set out some of those papers and markers she'd conned from Harry the mail clerk, in case anyone wanted to take some notes.

"Guess we're ready," she muttered, hoping to have a nice turnout. In reality, she doubted whether anyone would even bother showing up. Giving things a final check, she heard Clare's voice.

"Ready for the rush of inmates?"

Mattie snickered and said, "If two people come, it'll be a miracle." She had made a pitcher of sweet tea and put it in her little refrigerator. "It's so good to have you back, Clare, but you're back sooner than you thought. How come?"

"Those scary little munchkins turned into teen-agers. And that was even scarier!"

"Aw, Clare," Mattie said, mockingly; "where's the love?"

Her friend made a face and plopped into Mattie's chair. "How's your hand?"

"Nearly back to normal now." She showed Clare. "You can barely see anything."

They heard voices at Mattie's door, as Lillian, Kathy, Clint and some others showed up for her rally.

"Come in, come in!" Mattie said, eager to get things moving. "Thank you all for being here!" The others were chatting among themselves but Mattie got right down to business. She was about to make her opening blurb, when they heard a man's voice.

"Is this party for women only?" It was Bernard, of all people! With a cockeyed grin, he squawked, "Lemme' at 'em!"

Ignoring his "subtle" entrance, Mattie gave a shrug and said, "Come in, Bernard, and sit down. This rally is for everyone, but it's strictly business. Just close the door behind you."

Slumping, he whined, "I can't even get to first base with 'em," he said. Dejectedly, he took a seat on the edge of the bed, while one of the women hushed him.

Mattie started in. "How many of you are bored?" All hands went up. "How many of you feel you're being treated like losers?" Again, they all raised their hands. Now, for the big question, Mattie thought, taking a deep breath. "How many of you are willing to do something about it?"

She glanced around the room waiting for a response. There was none, other than Clare's.

"People, what is it you're afraid of?" Mattie asked; "the Autumn Leaves bogeyman?" That loosened them up a little, and then a woman named Gracie spoke.

"Mattie, you've only lived here a little while," she said; "the rest of us have been at Autumn Leaves for years. And we know how things are." Some of the others nodded in agreement. "Besides," she continued, "look at Salina Speers. She almost got the boot. If it wasn't for her daughter, who knows where she'd be now?"

"On the streets," Clint chimed in.

Gracie nodded, then sat back determinedly with her arms crossed and said, "Count me out."

Patiently, Mattie went on. "But that doesn't mean you can't change things, especially when we all feel we're not being treated properly." She gave a sigh and stopped being so nice. "Look," she began again, "we all have our own reasons for being here. But, Hell's bells! Are you all going to sit back like 'wussies' and let these people tell you how to live your lives?! Not me. I intend to do something about it!"

A murmur followed around the room. "But, Mattie," Lillian said, "what can we do?"

Mattie's "aha" moment had arrived. "Sign this," she said bluntly. She reached across her table and picked up a paper, which she read aloud. Basically, it was a petition that called for better food in the dining room, improved programs and a couple of other items in need of upgrading—for starters.

Then Mattie blurted, "I think the money we pay to cover our rent here at Autumn Leaves is being used to finance their vacations. But for the rest of us 'little people' it's the same old, same old. And I'm tired of it!" she added testily.

"But can you prove it, Mattie?" one of them asked half-accusingly.

"Well, no; not exactly. But I'll get proof. I do know Mr. Reemes has taken two cruises just in the short time I've lived here!" She was shaking her head. "But we have to let them know they can't bully us! After all, the rent money comes out of our pockets." She noticed a few heads nodding in agreement, as she went on. "Look, if all of us signed this petition, what would they do; kick all of us out? I doubt it! So, here goes."

And with that, Mattie put her signature at the very top of the list, and then passed the paper around to the others. "I don't know how or when, but some day they'll see this."

Again, Gracie piped up, which didn't help matters. "I ain't signin' nothin'," she said stubbornly. "I'm just thankful to have a roof over my head, and I ain't gonna' rock the boat!"

"Yeah, it's too risky," someone else said.

Mattie took a deep breath and calmed down. Then she headed for her refrigerator, brought out her cool sweet tea, and filled some small Styrofoam cups. Clare helped her pass them around.

They all chatted among themselves for a while and Mattie finished up the rally with a bit of advice. "Remember, people, if you don't get involved . . ."

"We know, Mattie, we know." It was Bernard who spoke. "If we don't get involved, we're part of the problem," he said. Then, to Mattie's surprise, he went ahead and signed the petition! Deep inside, she felt a little proud of him.

"Oh, by the way," Mattie said, smiling mischievously then, "one last thing. I'll be organizing another game in the yard soon. Anyone interested?"

They all laughed, even Gracie. "We'll be there, Mattie," Lillian assured her. "Right, people?"

A round of applause followed from the little group. Waving the petition, Mattie assured everyone she wouldn't let them down. "I'll stay on this," she said determinedly. And, she thought, at least I got them thinking!

As they gathered to leave, Mattie opened her door and thanked them once more. It was then that she noticed Gwen, who'd been standing in the hall by her door. Mattie turned to Clare and gave her a nudge. "There's Gwen. She's right" When they looked, Gwen had disappeared.

Clare snickered. "That woman moves faster than a greyhound in mating season."

Mattie tried to brush it off. "Oh, don't give 'Nosy-Posy' a second thought." Mattie decided she was going to visit that woman very soon and have a chat.

In all, Mattie gained only three signatures on the petition besides her own. "Shoulda served 'em some of my 'Harvey Ballwangers' instead of sweet tea," Clare said later; "they would've signed anything!"

After everyone left, Mattie made herself a cup of hot tea and sat at her little table. Actually she'd been a bit surprised by the turnout for the rally. Sipping her tea, she went over the whole get-together, replaying everyone's reactions, especially Gracie's. But Mattie didn't resent Gracie for speaking out. And, of course, she had no idea what the circumstances were that brought the woman to the center. This simply was the way things were for now.

Finishing her tea, Mattie told herself proudly it was the idea of the yard game that wrapped things up on a bright note. "Damn, I'm good!" she congratulated herself. With a smile, she gazed out her window and watched a couple of house finches working on a nest in the corner of the building.

The sound of her telephone ringing nearly startled Mattie, it was such a rarity. She heard Scotty's voice on the other end.

"Oh, Scotty; it's go good to hear from you! How are you?"

"Hey, Aunt Mattie! I'm doing great. In fact, I have some news for you."

"What, what? Tell me!"

"Well, I'm going to be coming down your way next week. Think you can put up with me again?"

"Don't be silly. Of course I can put up with you. I want to put up with you. So, how long will you be here?"

"Maybe for a long time. I'm moving down there."

His news startled Mattie. "Say what?!" she blurted. "Oh, that's wonderful! What brought this on?"

"I've done some research for my new computer shop. This area up here is fairly well saturated, so when I checked around the Asheville area, it looked promising. Anyway, I've gotta' run for now, but I'll call you when I get there, and I want to take you out for supper, okay?"

"'Okay' doesn't begin to cover it," she let him know. "Try 'wonderful'!"

He chuckled and said he'd talk to her soon, and they hung up. Mattie was so happy; she did a little dance around her room.

After Mattie shared the news about Scotty with Clare, they got to talking about the greenhouse. Mattie told Clare about the truck they'd sent out to pick up the glass and debris.

"I'm anxious to see how it looks, Clare. Come out there with me, okay?"

Clare sagged but knew it was useless to put up a fight. Heading out, they met up with Lillian and talked her into going with them.

"Girls, are you sure it's okay for us to be all the way out here?" Lillian asked cautiously, when they'd arrived.

"Oh, sure. We come here all the time; don't we, Clare? Clare?"

"Huh? Oh, yeah; right," she said.

The improvement around the greenhouse area was noticeable. Not only that, many of the surrounding tall weeds and jungle growth had been trampled down, probably by the truck.

But something else caught Mattie's eye. She nudged Clare. "That's new," she said quietly. Hanging on the door of the greenhouse frame was a makeshift sign that said, No Trespassing.

Mattie motioned for Clare to distract Lillian away from the sign. No sense in spooking the woman on her first visit. With her back to them, Mattie reached up, jiggled the sign loose, and then tossed it off. After all, she reasoned, this was part of Autumn Leaves' property and, as residents, they could be considered part owners—sort of.

"This would be a nice spot for us to grow some plants, don't you think?" Mattie asked the women. "If enough people were interested, we could make this our own little greenhouse." She looked at Clare for support. "Don't you agree, Clare?"

Clare drew back with a frown. "Girl, do I look like the type who'd hang around a greenhouse? Give me a break."

Lillian spoke up. "But you could learn about plants, Clare. What would be wrong with that?"

Clare rolled her eyes, and Mattie gave Lillian an approving nod. Mattie was encouraged. She felt certain that, some day, they could put the greenhouse to their own use. She'd seen it happen in other areas, a sort of "community garden," where the gardeners each had their own space and maintained it themselves.

Yes, she decided, the idea would be worth pursuing. And pursue it she would.

Back in her room, Mattie stretched out in her lounge chair and thought about the recent events. She felt a little proud of herself for being so bold as to hold the protest rally. After all, what if Mr. Reemes or Mr. Prescott had come to her room and found the other residents there! They'd suspect something right away (not that she couldn't have a party if she wanted to). It would just be without Reemes' permission! But, it could've been risky. And the last thing she wanted was to get any of the others in trouble.

Regardless, Mattie was used to taking chances. She learned years ago that in order to get results, you sometimes had to face risks. Like the time she worked as an associate at a small bank in a Cleveland suburb. Just before the bank was closing for the day, she heard the sound of a man's voice, loudly ordering people around. She gasped at seeing a guy wearing a ski mask, standing in the empty lobby, with his back to her office and a gun aimed at the tellers.

Mattie was witnessing a robbery! "The money! Gimme the money!" he'd shouted.

Her first impulse was to snatch up a nearby fire extinguisher. Without thinking of the consequences, she headed for the lobby, ran right up behind the robber and with the extinguisher aimed at the guy's head, brazenly yelled, "How about this instead?!" And she turned the thing on him, dousing him with foam, while one of the tellers set off an alarm. At that point, a customer jumped the guy and held him down until the police arrived.

Remembering the episode, Mattie gave a shrug. "Risky, yes," she muttered; "smart, no!" But it was what she felt she had to do at the time.

Then there was the greenhouse, or at least that's what Mattie liked to call it. At this point, it was obviously nothing more than a rusty metal frame with a door, a bunch of weeds, and a discarded *No Trespassing* sign. She wondered what the reason was for the sign, but soon realized that a posted sign got Autumn Leaves off the hook, in case Mattie was considering a lawsuit from when she cut her hand.

Shaking her head, she let out a long sigh. "There's always something," she muttered, before closing her eyes and dozing off.

Mary A. Berger

A few days later, Mattie slipped into her purple jogging suit and ran through some exercises, pausing now and then to take in a couple of deep breaths. Her routine was interrupted by the phone ringing and, once again, she heard Scotty's voice on the other end. They chatted briefly, and then he said, "I'll be over around five. How's that sound?"

"Five o'clock tonight? You mean you're down here, already?!" she squawked.

"Yup. And I'll pick you up later, young lady," he told her.

After hanging up, Mattie could barely conceal her joy. "I've got a da-ate, I've got a da-ate," she sang. Then she went to her little closet and thought about what to wear. "Let's see... oh, this pink pants suit will be good, with my beige sandals. Yes, that'll look nice." She hummed to herself as she laid out the suit on her bed and set the shoes beneath it on the floor.

Scotty arrived a little early to pick her up. Wearing black jeans, cowboy boots and a black and grey striped sports shirt, he greeted her at the door to her room. After exchanging a huge hug, they both wanted to talk at the same time.

"Wait, wait," Mattie said, giggling. "Let's save the talk for dinner."

Just then Lauren stepped into Mattie's room. "Mrs. Morgan, I was just leav—" She saw Scotty and began apologizing. "Oh, I'm sorry; I had no idea y'all had a guest."

"He's no guest, Lauren; this is my nephew, Scotty. Scotty, I'd like you to meet Lauren. She does everything around here," Mattie said beaming.

Scotty could only stare at Lauren. Mattie caught it and said to him, "Well, don't just stand there. Say something."

It was Lauren who spoke. "Hello, Scotty." Her deep brown eyes seemed almost glowing, when she extended her warm hand to his. "It's nice to meet y'all."

"Aunt Mattie," Scotty said, without taking his eyes off Lauren, "Autumn Leaves just got better."

With a charming laugh, Lauren excused herself, and said she'd talk to Mattie tomorrow. Scotty's gaze followed Lauren all the way out the door and into the hallway. Then, with cocker spaniel puppy eyes, he murmured, "Wowww."

Mattie gave a little snort. "Are we leaving, or are you just going to stand there drooling?"

Scotty had chosen a nice chalet style restaurant out by Lake Julian. With its soaring wood fireplace, oak rafters, big picture windows that overlooked the lake, it took Mattie's breath away. Inside, she caught the unmistakable aroma of steaks grilling. "Oh, this smells heavenly!" she said, inhaling deeply.

"I hear the steaks are awesome!" commented Scotty.

With Scotty's hand on Mattie's shoulder, a hostess led them to a corner booth, where they each ordered a glass of white wine.

"How'd you find this place, Scotty?"

"Computer," he said. "And you'd be surprised how well recommended it was when I checked for ratings. You can find all that stuff on a computer, you know," he told her, his eyes lighting up. "But you know a little about computers, don't you, Aunt Mattie?"

"Oh, sure; I used one back in the landscaping office. I have a bit of background on them. Why?"

"Just wondering."

After a while, she said, "Scotty, you have no idea how much this outing means to me."

She reached over and patted his hand, as their wine arrived. "So, anything new with the estate?" she asked.

"Oh, yes. Actually, there is." They both raised their glasses in a toast, and Scotty filled her in on the latest. "Jed has a new lead on Owen Black. He heard about it just before I flew down this afternoon."

"Oh?"

"Yeah, they think they know where Black is."

"Really? Well, if they can find him, they'll find Eva." Sipping the wine, she glanced at Scotty. "Right?"

He gave a sarcastic sniff. "That's the problem. He's supposedly alone."

"What?! I don't understand."

Scotty shrugged and said this was all Jed knew right now. "He'll probably be calling you tonight. He wanted me to let you know, since I was coming to see you. In fact," Scotty went on, "Jed said he'd probably be coming down this way again in a few weeks. He'll fill you in when he calls."

Mattie was delighted, took a couple more sips of her wine, and wondered what the significance was of finding Owen Black alone. But maybe Owen would let them know when they caught up with him.

"Actually, Jed said he might come down even sooner. Right now, everything's kind of up in the air. He's been so busy with his practice. But I know for a fact, your case is number one on his list."

It made Mattie feel good to think she was number one on someone's list, besides that of Mr. Reemes!

They both ordered prime rib with salad and baked potato, and chatted all through dinner.

"Delicious!" Mattie said, pushing away her plate at the end of the meal. "But the best part is just being away from Autumn Leaves and here with you."

Scotty grew thoughtful. "Uh, Aunt Mattie, about that Lauren girl I met earlier; is she...um...taken?" Trying to appear nonchalant by pushing around some scraps on his plate with his fork, he avoided Mattie's eyes.

"If you mean as in 'married', no. And I don't think she's seeing anyone right now. She's been a lifesaver to me. Wonderful girl." Mattie watched Scotty's eyes light up at the mention of Lauren's name and the fact that she was single, and she smiled to herself.

Later, when they returned to the center, Scotty told her he had to get something from the trunk of the car. She watched him lift out a narrow briefcase.

"Don't tell me you're going to set up shop here at Autumn Leaves?"

"Nope. Just wanted to show you something." He looked pleased with himself.

They strolled down the hall until they reached Mattie's room and, of course, she had him come in. She kicked off her shoes, while Scotty searched around for a wall socket. Then he took a computer and cord from the briefcase, plugged it in and started it up.

Mattie stood looking over his shoulder. "Nice computer. Kinda small, isn't it?"

"It's a laptop, and it's all yours" he told her, beaming. "I'll get you set up so you can send email and go online." His big grin told her he was proud of himself.

"What, you mean I'll be able to email you, or Jed, or my friends in Asheville, or Cleveland?!"

"Yup. Soon as you get everyone's addresses."

Mattie couldn't believe it. "Scotty, you are a sneak," she teased, "but computers are expensive. Let me pay."

"No way! Besides, this thing was going to be trashed," he explained; "but I worked on it and, instead of putting it in my shop, I thought maybe you'd like to use it!"

"Would I!" She sat right down and began pounding away. "You'll have to show me all the ins and outs," she said. "Oh, thank you Scotty; thank you so much."

"Just play around with it for a while," he said, "and I'll come back and show you some shortcuts and stuff, okay? And I found a printer for you, too." Her eyes danced with excitement at hearing that. Scotty checked the time. "Look, I've gotta' run and meet up with a real estate guy. We have some places to check out."

He planted another one of his big smooches on her cheek, and she thanked him again for the wonderful evening. Watching him walk away, Mattie counted her blessings. Then she plopped in her lounge chair and waited for Jed's call.

Jed called, just like he'd told Scotty he would. Mattie picked up the phone and they started right in with their usual easy conversation. "I want to get down there to see you again, Mattie," Jed told her warmly. Mattie could almost see his wonderful smile in his voice.

Then she switched the conversation to Scotty's message about Owen Black. "Jed, tell me, what's this I hear about that creepy lawyer of mine?"

Jed didn't really slough off her question, yet he wasn't exactly talkative either. "Oh well, we'll talk more about that when I'm there." Mattie had the feeling he was keeping something from her, or at least, not telling her everything.

"Oh, yes; Scotty told me you'd be coming down this way again. I'm really looking forward to it."

"I was going to wait 'til the end of the month," he told her, "when most of my cases will be finished up. My partner is on special assignment but my assistant, Kathy, can handle things. She's very capable. Besides," he added with a chuckle, "I'd rather be there. Would it be all right if I come down next week?" Of course, she agreed, smiling.

When Mattie went to bed that night, she found herself thinking about Jed's next visit. It made her a little uneasy that he seemed to be putting her off about discussing Owen Black. She convinced herself that he probably just didn't want to go into details over the phone. She yawned, and then gave a sigh. It had been so good to talk to Jed. She didn't know what she would have done over these past few months if it weren't for him.

She remembered his first wife, Ruth, who'd moved to Cleveland after having spent much of her life in Massachusetts. Although she was an attractive brunette with big brown eyes, she struck Mattie as a loner, who frowned a lot and seemed to enjoy the company of her sewing more than Jed's. Gabe and Mattie had even joined them for dinner a few times, but neither could really warm up to her. She died at a fairly young age shortly after marrying Jed. Mattie felt a little sorry for him after that;

he'd always seemed so lonely. Regardless, Mattie was truly thankful for his help now.

Then, a frightening thought stabbed her and her eyes opened wide. This was the first day she hadn't thought about Gabe once. Not once! She laid back, drew the covers up around her, and let the tears flow. Dabbing at her eyes with a tissue, she began to look back on some of the good times she and Gabe had had together. Smiling then, as memories of the old Victorian mansion flooded her mind; she plumped her pillow and fell asleep.

The next morning, Mattie decided to pay Gwen a visit. Something about that woman rubbed her the wrong way, felt out of kilter, like wearing high heels to aerobics class.

When she arrived at Gwen's room, she knocked on the door, which was slightly ajar. No response. After knocking a little harder, the door swung open just wide enough for Mattie to see Gwen sprawled out cold on her bed with a bottle of alcohol in one hand.

"Whoa, what's this?" Mattie murmured, with her eyes big as melons. Cautiously, she stepped into Gwen's room and shook her arm lightly. Gwen responded with a short grunt and rolled over on her other side. Mattie gave a sigh of relief and murmured, "At least you're alive."

She noticed a couple of empty bottles poking out from under the bed. Her curiosity got the best of her. She took a closer look beneath the bed and saw at least a dozen or more empty ones, strewn about.

Mattie let out a low whistle of surprise. Then, glancing around, she saw an unopened bottle on the nightstand and spotted a piece of paper tucked under it. Peering over her shoulder to make sure no one saw her, she slipped the paper out. There was something written on it. Thanks for your help. She heard voices in the hall and hastily crammed the note in her pocket. After waiting a moment, she peeked out and saw the hall was clear.

"I'm outta' here!" she muttered, closing Gwen's door and heading for Clare's.

"Girl, you are totally freaked out," Clare told her on hearing about Gwen. She led Mattie to a chair and had her sit down. "Don't worry, Mattie; I've seen several of the inmates here seriously boozing it up. Really, some of these people are nothing but lushes." With a shrug, Clare added, "That's all they know. And Autumn Leaves is all they can afford."

"I know, Clare. It's just that after I saw the note"

"Note? What note?"

"Oh, I was so upset I forgot to tell you." Mattie dug into her pocket and pulled out the wrinkled piece of paper. "This," she said, handing it to Clare.

"Thanks for your help." Clare drew back, frowning. "What the?" She and Mattie stared at each other, trying to make sense out of the words.

"Yeah. Now you know why I was upset."

"Something's going on here, Mattie. I smell a rat with 'Mr. Reemes' tattooed on its rear end."

Mattie frowned and said, "I had the same feeling, Clare. Lord above, what're we going to do?"

After a moment, Clare said, "Didn't you say Jed was coming to see you next week?" Mattie nodded. "Why don't you show him this note and tell him about Gwen? Just to get his reaction."

Mattie nodded again. "Okay." She folded the note and put it back in her pocket. "Thanks, Clare. You've been a big help. Honestly, I don't know what I'd do without you."

After Mattie tucked the note safely away in the kitchen cupboard, she sat in her lounge chair sipping some tea. Thoughts of the note kept running through her mind. If it had been written by Mr. Reemes, what was the point? Paying off Gwen with alcohol? Paying her off for what? Then it hit her. She'd seen Gwen several times, listening at Mattie's door, acting suspiciously, disappearing on a moment's notice. Had she been reporting to Mr. Reemes?!

"That little snitch!" Mattie muttered. "I won't stand for this! I'm going right back there and wake that woman up! I don't care if she is out cold." She set her teacup in the sink and headed back to Gwen's. "We're going to put a stop to this right now!"

When she got there, Mattie felt more than a little riled up; she was fuming. Knocking hard on Gwen's door, she paused, and then knocked harder.

"Wh-what? Who'sh there?" Mattie heard Gwen say, almost with a moan.

"It's Mattie. Mattie Morgan. I'd like to talk to you." And with that, Mattie stepped into the room. She saw Gwen in a pitiful state, sitting semi-upright, her hair mussed and her eyes not focusing properly. "Lord above," Mattie murmured. Was Gwen one of the lushes Clare told her about?! Her anger disappeared as she approached Gwen and watched her struggling to sit up, her tongue hanging loosely.

"Who, who're you? Wha d'you want?" Gwen asked frowning, her words slurred.

Mattie sat beside her on the bed and spoke quietly. "I'm Mattie. I just wanted to talk to you, Gwen." She looked around the room and saw a pot of coffee still warm on a hot plate.

Finding a cup, she poured some coffee into it, brought it to Gwen, and sat down again. "Here, have some of this. It'll make you feel better." She steadied the cup and helped Gwen get some of the liquid inside.

After a few moments had passed, and Gwen had consumed more of the coffee, she could sit up without Mattie's help.

"I must look awful," Gwen said, hesitantly.

Mattie nodded and smiled. "You sure do." After Gwen finished the coffee, Mattie took the cup and set it aside. "Would you like to wash up a bit or splash some cold water on your face?"

Gwen simply stared at her. "Why're you bein' so nice t'me?" she asked, her words still loose.

"Well, you looked like you could use some help. Let me know if there's anything more I can do." Mattie started to get up, but Gwen reached out tentatively and put her hand on Mattie's arm.

"Don't go," she said.

Stunned, Mattie replied, "All right. I'll stay for just a minute."

Suddenly, Gwen burst into tears and hid her face in her hands. "I'm so ashamed!" she blurted out.

"Because you were out like a light?" Mattie asked, not exactly sure where things were going at that point.

"Yeah," Gwen said, sniffling. "But mostly because...because he wanted me to spy on you!" Next thing Mattie knew, Gwen threw her arms around Mattie's shoulders and sobbed like a child. "I didn't want...to spy but he told me if I helped him (sniff) he'd get me some booze!" Flabbergasted, Mattie held her until she stopped crying.

Finally, she asked, "Who promised you, Gwen? Who was it?"

Suddenly Gwen drew back, terrified, and sucked in a big breath. "Oh, no; I wasn't s'posed to tell! Oh, I'll be in big trouble. You better go now, Mattie."

"Don't worry, Gwen," Mattie tried to reassure her; "it'll be all right.

"No, it won't!"

Mattie patted her hand, got up and started for the door, when from behind she heard Gwen's soft words, "Mattie...thank you."

The impact of what had just taken place jarred Mattie. Outside in the hall, she leaned against the wall, steadying herself, trying to take it all in. She inhaled a couple of deep breaths, and then headed outdoors. Walking would help.

The morning sun shone brightly and the birds were singing. But she didn't notice. All that mattered was the visit with Gwen and how she had opened up to Mattie, putting her arms around Mattie's neck, of all things! And crying! Strolling along, however, as Mattie gave it more thought, she was convinced the sudden change in Gwen was no doubt due to the affects of the alcohol. After a while, she even smiled to herself. Of course, she thought with a smirk, why else would Gwen have changed so suddenly—and so dramatically.

After a while, she turned and strolled back to the center. Now she heard the birds, felt the warm sun on her shoulders, and sent up a prayer of thanks for helping put things in perspective.

Back in her room, Mattie decided it was time to plan another outdoors game. She smiled, remembering how she and the neighbor kids used to play touch football when they were young. Now if only she could get her hands on a football. Wouldn't that frost Mr. Reemes' pumpkin, she thought with a chuckle; seeing the "inmates" in a round of touch football. She imagined he'd be a basket case.

After a while, she fixed a bowl of chicken rice soup with soda crackers, and then made tea. Finishing her lunch, she went to her computer and began planning for her next game day. "Let the games begin!" she said, chuckling, while checking the calendar and entering her plans. "I need to have another rally, too," she reminded herself.

Mattie had been so preoccupied with her scheduling that she didn't hear Clare calling to her.

"Mattie? Oh, good; you're here." Mattie glanced up as Clare stepped into her room.

"What's happening, Clare?"

Clare was frowning. "It's Gwen," she said. "They're taking her to the hospital."

Mattie felt a mild tremor run through her body. "What?"

"Lauren was in Gwen's room just a while ago," Clare explained, sitting on the edge of Mattie's bed. "She couldn't get a pulse, so she called 911. But the paramedics brought her back, and they were getting her ready to go to the hospital when I was there. I heard them say she'd probably had way too much to drink. So they want to keep her overnight for observation."

The two women embraced for a moment, and then Mattie told Clare about her visit with Gwen.

"She actually put her arms around you, and cried?" Clare asked in disbelief. "No way!"

"Yes, she did. But it was what she told me, about somebody wanting her to keep tabs on me. That was the kicker, Clare."

"I think we both know who's behind that."

"Oh, sure. But you can't prove it." Mattie looked disgusted. "Imagine, taking advantage of someone that way. How awful!"

"You still have that note, right?"

Mattie nodded. "Yes. I stashed it in with my teabags in the cupboard."

Clare snickered. "Make sure you don't use it for a tea bag."

Mattie smiled and shook her head. "Whew! What a day this turned out to be." Then she turned to her friend. "Clare, got any more of that 'orange juice'?"

"Follow me," Clare said, grinning.

In Clare's room, the two friends flopped in chairs with their drinks. "I just hope Gwen makes it," Mattie said, letting out a long sigh.

"Me, too. I knew Gwen drank a little, but I didn't realize how bad things were. I mean, she always keeps to herself. And she acts so weird."

"I know. But Gwen's last words to me—thanking me— I'll never forget that!"

Clare could only stare at her friend in admiration. "Mattie?" she finally blurted out; "how can anyone as pushy and nosy as you be so damned likeable?"

Mattie gave a little shrug and said, tongue in cheek, "Guess it's just part of my magnetic personality." And she rolled her eyes and laughed.

Snickering, Clare said, "Have some more 'orange juice'."

The next day, Mattie was right back at her computer, when a knock on the door stirred her. Looking up, she saw Clint, the guy who'd been at the awful weed lecture weeks before.

"Hey, Mattie. Can I come in for a minute?"

"Of course. Come on in, Clint." She also recalled that he'd attended her first protest rally. "What's on your mind?"

"Uh, well...I've been hearing some rumors. About the guys who run things here, and I just wanted to talk to you, if it's okay."

He had Mattie's immediate attention. "Absolutely. Talk."

He folded his arms and leaned against her table. "For one thing, I gave a lot of thought to what you said at your rally; about how they're usin' our money for their own fun 'stead of puttin' it here in this center where we need it." His eyes narrowed then. "That ain't right. It just ain't right."

"I'm listening," Mattie said. At that point, her curiosity was running at speed-of-sound level.

"And I've been hearin' something about them boys getting liquor for the people here who like to booze it up, just to keep 'em in their place." Mattie's eyes were the size of melons. "Nobody thinks Mr. Bates is part of it, though," Clint was quick to add. "It's just Reemes—and whoever else works for him, or with him." He looked down at the floor. "I'm pretty sure this has been goin' on for a while, but it ain't been this bad, 'til now. Besides, nobody wants to be a snitch, y'know what I'm sayin'?"

Mattie nodded. Word did indeed spread fast at Autumn Leaves. And now Clint was telling her about some of the other residents being involved in the bribery thing, as well. "But what can I do?" she asked innocently, while feeling inside like a race horse at the starting gate, barely able to hold herself back, but still wanting the words to come from him.

Clint scratched his head. "Well, some of us were thinkin' maybe, well, maybe we could get you to have another one of those rallies like you did before and—"

"I'd be more than happy to!" she squealed. Then she asked, "Clint, have you been hearing these stories from any of the other folks around here?"

"Hell, yeah," he answered quickly. "But we thought maybe you could—"

Mattie glanced at her computer screen. "Is tomorrow afternoon, say two o'clock, soon enough?"

Clint let out a quick breath. "You don't waste any time, do you?"

"Just pass the word around," she told him. "We'll see what we can do."

After he left, Mattie let out a subdued "Hoo-ha!" and pumped her fist. This was exactly what she'd been hoping for, getting some of the other inmates off their backsides and showing an interest in their own welfare. Too bad it took the incident with Gwen to make it happen.

Still, Mattie felt energized beyond words. Then she got busy, hastily making up new flyers, planning to get them out first thing next morning.

"We could slip them inside people's newspapers," Clare suggested, after Mattie told her about the visit from Clint.

"Clare, you're a genius! That's a great idea!" she told her friend, giving her a big hug. "Meet you in the hall first thing tomorrow morning."

Mary A. Berger

 8

Mattie's timing for her next rally couldn't have been better. Apparently word about Gwen had spread like a case of measles. Mattie wondered how everyone heard about it so fast. Granted, someone could have caught Gwen the same way Mattie did—in her almost-sober-but-still-a-little-bombed state. So Gwen, herself, might have helped spread the word about "helping" Reemes, or whoever, in return for the alcohol. In a way, Mattie could understand the residents not wanting to squeal on each other, but the thing with Gwen might well have been the last straw for them.

Rally day arrived. While rinsing her lunch dishes, Mattie heard the sounds of people's voices approaching. She glanced at her watch. "Two o'clock, already?!" There was no time for setting out some cookies or making tea or anything because people were streaming into her room, one by one. Clare even brought along her little footstool in case Mattie needed it.

By the time Mattie greeted everyone, her jaw dropped. Close to thirty people! All crammed into her little room! In a rare moment, Mattie was speechless. Clare had to nudge her. "C'mon, Matts; let's get this monkey moving!"

"Oh, right!" Mattie stepped up onto Clare's footstool in the middle of the room, while Clare clanged on a glass with a spoon.

"People! People!" she called out; "let's hear what Mattie has to say."

Mattie got right to the point. "First of all, I'm tickled to see so many of you! Now let's talk about why we're here. As you all know, we still have some problems." A murmur of agreement went around the room. "First off, you've probably all heard about Gwen being rushed to the hospital." In unison, sounds of concern followed as Mattie continued. "Now I'm pretty sure Gwen had a little 'help' with her drinking problem. And some of us are wondering if that 'help' didn't come from the folks who run this place." Mattie paused, waiting for cries of shock or surprise, which didn't happen. Amazingly, what followed was a more a show of outrage.

"We all knew about that!" one woman called out. "It's terrible! I mean, Gwen isn't exactly the friendly type, but she doesn't deserve to be treated that way." Several others shook their heads in disgust.

"I think we need to let the people who run Autumn Leaves know how upset we are!" To Mattie's astonishment, it was Lillian speaking up. "We can't go on like this," Lillian continued. "Nearly everyone here knows some of the folks have drinking problems, but plying them with more liquor to manipulate them, or to keep them quiet. That's awful! And I'm sick of living this way!"

A hefty round of applause followed, but then one of the men, Neil, spoke up. "You all sound like you want Autumn Leaves to be perfect," he said. "We can't expect that. After all, none of us can get out of here, most likely, so we're pretty much stuck under someone else's control, and things are probably never going to be the way we think they should."

"Nothing is ever perfect," Mattie said. "But one thing's for sure: if we allow ourselves to be walked over, like a bunch of stale marshmallows, that's exactly what will happen." She glanced around the room and quipped, "I don't see any stale marshmallows here, do you?"

"Just a couple of stubborn mules," Neil came back.

"That's exactly what we need!" Mattie said, laughing along with the others.

Clint spoke then. "I think it's time for all of us to take stock of what's been goin' on at Autumn Leaves. Nobody wants to rock the boat, or speak up—nobody 'cept Mattie, that is."

A round of applause followed his remarks. Mattie brushed it all off good-naturedly. "What we need to do," she told them, "is to get organized." She stepped down, went to her kitchen and opened a drawer, then pulled out the petition from her first rally. "For those of you who couldn't attend our first get-together," she said, "here's a list of concerns that I think need to be addressed." Mattie read off a few. "The list goes on, but the problem is, we could only get a couple of signatures. So if the rest of you feel this is important, I need your John Henry. And I guarantee this petition will reach either Mr. Reemes or Mr. Prescott—or both."

"Who?" and "Who's that?" and "Who's Mr. Prescott?" could be heard around the room.

Mattie sagged. "He owns Autumn Leaves. You mean you've never met him?"

They all looked at each other, shrugged and shook their heads. "I never heard of him," someone said. "How'd you meet him, Mattie?"

"How does Mattie do *anything?!*" Clare said with a spurt of laughter. Then she offered to pass the petition around for everyone to look at.

Mattie watched as several people wrote their names. By the time she had it back in her hands, she saw that nearly everyone present had signed it. She let out a hoot of victory before saying, "Now that's what I'm talkin' about! Thank you, thank you, everyone!"

By the end of the rally, they had all decided to call themselves "The Partners," and to form a smaller group known as their "Agents" to represent them. The Agents would choose a day when Mr. Reemes was in the center ("...when he's not off on a cruise!" Mattie snapped), then they would quickly round each other up, go to his office and hit him head on with the petition. "That way," Mattie said, "with four or five of us going together, he won't be so likely to blow us off." She looked around the room at the others. "Sound logical?"

Everyone nodded in agreement. "As long as you're one of the Agents who goes to see him," someone told Mattie.

"I'll gladly volunteer for the job, and don't worry," Mattie assured them with a mischievous smile, "I know the way to his office."

After everyone left, Mattie sat in her chair and thought about the rally. She was close to dozing off, when she heard a tap on her door. She looked around to see Hank, the groundskeeper. "Hey, Miss Mattie. I brought you a little somethin'." Her eyes opened wide with delight, when he handed her a wooden bird feeder.

"Where'd you get this?" she asked. "Don't tell me you made it!"

"Yes, ma'am. Made it from some old wood left over from one of the trees they cut down, out by your greenhouse."

"It's beautiful, Hank! Thank you so much." She especially liked the sound of *her* greenhouse. "I love watching the birds. I'll try to hang it outside my window soon."

"Reckon I could do it for you," he offered.

Again, Mattie was appreciative. "You're too kind," she let him know. "Thanks so much."

Before turning away, a big grin crept over his face. "Say, Miss Mattie, did you hear the one about the woman who was taking her little boy to church? She asks him, 'Why is it important to be quiet in church? And the boy says, 'Because everybody's sleeping?'"

Mattie gave a hearty laugh and said, "You need to come inside this center more often."

"Oh, I could go on for hours," he informed her, beaming.

"Is that right?" said Mattie. "Well, I'll have to remember that." And Mattie filed that fact back in a little corner of her memory bank and thanked him again.

Mary A. Berger

9

A few days later, Mattie was looking forward to another visit from Jed. He picked up Scotty on his way to see Mattie and, of course, she was tickled.

"Mattie," Jed almost crooned, taking her into his arms when he and Scotty arrived, "you look marvelous!" He held her at arm's length. "How do you do it? The rest of us get older but you just stay beautiful." He faked a pout. "It's not fair."

"It has to be these palatial surroundings," she went along, good-naturedly. "And the food here is beyond belief! So appetizing and nutritious. Mmm," she said sarcastically, while licking her lips. Then she fell into Scotty's arms, while he snatched her up in his usual way, swung her around, and gave her one of his big smooches.

The early June day was too hot and sticky to sit outside on the porch, so they stayed in Mattie's room to visit. Besides, the big old black bees were dive-bombing those who set foot outdoors, so that was their main incentive to stay put.

Mattie set out a pitcher of cool sweet tea and had a small oscillating fan going, which at least helped move the muggy air around. The guys were wearing short-sleeved golf shirts and Bermudas, and Mattie had on a tank top with cropped denims, so they were fairly comfortable.

"What about your computer place, Scotty? Or an apartment? Have you found anything?" Mattie asked.

"Sure have. It's south of Asheville, near Mountain Home. Ever hear of it?"

"I think so. Pretty area, not too built up yet?"

"Right. But since they expanded the highway, things will start taking off soon." He took a swallow of tea. "Anyway, I'm renting a small house about a block away from my computer place. Started up the shop about two weeks ago. And you know how it is in the computer business; you take each day one byte at a time."

Jed and Mattie let out groans at the pun, and Jed turned to her. "So, Mattie," he said, after taking more of the refreshing drink, "how are you getting along?" His warm blue eyes looked into hers. "I've really missed you. Can you stand it to stay here? We could put you up at an inn or"

Mattie waved him off. "No, that sounds boring. But thanks, Jed. Besides, I have some work that needs to be done here." She told them about the rally, and about how they came up with the titles of Partners and Agents. Then she mentioned Gwen and her situation.

Jed sounded concerned. "You really think someone's taking advantage of her drinking problem, Mattie?"

"Oh, the note!" She jumped out of her chair and retrieved the note she'd saved to show Jed.

After looking it over carefully, he gave a shrug and said, "This certainly doesn't look good. Too bad no one signed it." He opened his billfold and tucked the folded note inside. "Mind if I keep this? You just never know." Of course, Mattie agreed.

Scotty chuckled and poured himself some more tea. "Aunt Mattie, your work is never done, anyone can see that," he said, after hearing about her rally. "I think they could use you in the sheriff's department." And he went into a routine where Mattie growls, "Okay, you druggie scumbags; hands up! It's Mattie Morgan!" and she draws a pistol from each hip. They all laughed, while Scotty dubbed her Deputy Mattie.

Jed grew serious then. "I think we told you they found Owen Black?" Mattie nodded. "He was holed up, penniless, in some cheap, back street rooming house on San Juan; and locating him was a piece of cake. Several of the islanders had seen him emptying trash and doing menial jobs in return for his room and board there."

Mattie was all ears. "Did he say where Eva was?"

After a brief hesitation, Jed said, "No, he didn't. But he did tell the authorities he and Eva had planned to go off together and live an islander's life, on the money Eva got from your estate." He looked troubled. "That's about all we know at this point. I wish I had better news but we'll keep at it."

"But I thought once you got your hands on Owen, he'd squeal like a pig!" Mattie said, refreshing their drinks.

Jed shook his head. "He insists he doesn't know where Eva is. And strangely enough, I tend to believe him. He told the authorities that they'd dreamed up this scheme even before they boarded the cruise ship. Their plan was to put their barest essentials in small bags at the last stop of their cruise, and leave the ship with Eva's money in hand, which Black says she simply put into a checking account. Then they were going to spend the rest of their lives on the island."

"That doesn't sound like Eva," Mattie said, frowning. "She doesn't fit into that lifestyle."

Jed had to agree. "And I doubt she's made any investments. I don't think she knows the first thing about managing money. Anyway, on the final day of the cruise they went ashore. Everything was going as planned until Eva told Owen she wanted to do some shopping. Owen hung around a restaurant where they were supposed to meet up later, but he claims Eva never came back. He says he waited for hours and even checked with the local police in case something might have happened to her."

Scotty said, "Well, it makes sense that if Eva had the money and dumped Black, he wouldn't know where she was." He made a low grumbling sound. "I wouldn't put it past her, knowing her. She no doubt intended to get rid of him in the first place. She's probably living high off the hog . . . somewhere."

"There's one thing that keeps me hopeful," Jed told them. "Eva's not very, uh, bright.

His comment made Mattie howl. "Bright like a wilted sunflower!"

"But that's the thing, Mattie. She's not the kind of person who has the know-how or the imagination to get very far, so I doubt she'd do anything rash. She just doesn't fit the profile. She might try but, honestly, I don't think she's capable." He looked her in the eye. "Remember, money can't buy class."

"You're right, there, Jed." She sighed. "I thought when you got here, maybe you were going to tell me you'd found Eva and—"

Jed's warm hand held hers and he assured her they were doing all they could for now. "They're bringing Owen back here for questioning," he said. "We've got to get to the bottom of what happened with the will and all of Gabe's papers."

"I told you Eva already had a new car, didn't I?" Mattie asked.

"Must've been a rental," Scotty said; "or she wouldn't have just up and left it."

"And I have no idea what she did with my car," Mattie said.

"Probably got rid of it on the underground," Scotty told her.

Jed's chin jutted out determinedly, while disgust crept over his face. "Owen and Eva will pay for what they've done, Mattie. You can be sure of that." He could only stare at her, his eyes filled with compassion and sympathy . . . and more.

"I know that, Jed," she told him. "I trust you completely." He held her hand, while the two of them gazed at each other for a brief moment.

Scotty picked up on it and joked, "You two want to be alone?"

Mattie actually blushed when he said that. "Scotty, we're just good friends!"

At that moment, Lauren stepped into the room but stopped abruptly at seeing Scotty and Jed. "Oh, Mrs. Morgan, I'm sorry. I seem to keep barging in when y'all have company."

Scotty was on his feet shaking Lauren's hand vigorously and saying how great it was to see her again, while Mattie introduced her to Jed.

"Lauren, I haven't seen you in a while," Mattie told her. "I hope everything's all right."

Lauren squeezed Mattie's shoulders warmly. "Oh, there's been a lot going on lately, and you probably heard about Gwen."

"Yes. How's she doing, have you heard?"

"She should be coming back later this week, poor thing."

Poor thing, indeed, Mattie thought but said only, "Well, we'll all be watching for her to get back." Mattie invited

Lauren to join them around her little table, and she went to make more tea. As before, Scotty seemed lost in Lauren's presence, unable to take his eyes off her. And Mattie noticed Lauren was smiling more than usual as she chatted with him.

On her way back with the tea, Mattie couldn't resist repeating Scotty's earlier remark, murmuring aside to him, "You two want to be alone?" Scotty could barely hold back a grin.

Just as they were getting into a nice conversation, Lauren heard herself being paged. She slumped and apologized. "Gotta' go, folks. I'm sorry." As she got up from her chair, she shook Jed's hand and said something pleasant, then turned to Scotty and drawled sweetly, "I do hope I'll see y'all again, Scotty."

Jed and Mattie smiled at each other, watching Scotty watching her as she left the room.

"Scotty," Mattie finally said. "Why don't you ask her out? I think she'd like that."

"Really?"

"Of course. I saw the way she was looking at you."

That was all Scotty needed to hear. He bounced from his chair, and hightailed it out of the room to catch up with Lauren.

"They'd make a nice couple, wouldn't they?" Mattie said, smiling at Jed. He was looking straight at her, his eyes intense. "Wouldn't they?" she repeated.

"Mattie...if there's ever anything you need, you know I'd do all I could to see that you get it. And..." He seemed to be searching for the right words. He rested his elbow on the table and propped his chin in his hand, still looking into her eyes. "...I know it hasn't been long since you lost

Gabe," he went on, "but I..." His voice grew low and tender as he confessed, "...Mattie...I'm crazy about you."

She blew a puff of air into that springy curl that hung down. "You are?"

"Yes. I am." Looking at her lovingly, he said, "But I don't want to rush you, or make you feel uncomfortable."

"Jed, I don't know what to say. I adore you, but I don't know if I'm ready"

Leaning closer, he took her hand in his. "Don't say anything more right now. I just had to let you know how I feel." His blue eyes were glowing. And for the second time that week, Mattie was speechless.

A noisy "Ya-hoo!"from Scotty interrupted their close moment. In fact, they heard it in the hall even before he showed up. When he came in the room, he cried out, "She said yes!" He pumped his fist and strutted around the room. "She's going out with me! Su-weet!" He flopped into his chair, one hand over his heart. "This is so freakin' awesome! I'm so glad you live here! I never would've met—" He caught himself, and began apologizing to Mattie. "Oh, wait; I didn't really mean that, Aunt Mattie. What I meant was—"

"I think you're in love, you big dope!" Mattie said, grinning and squeezing his arm. "Seriously, Scotty; I'm glad you and Lauren are hooking up. It's wonderful." Just then, Jed's cell phone rang.

While Jed answered it, Scotty took a big breath, squared himself, and changed the subject. Trying to appear more casual, he asked Mattie, "By the way, how's that computer working out?"

"Oh, I meant to mention that," she said. "When you get a chance, I could use some more help getting some email stuff started." Of course, Scotty agreed and said he'd come back that weekend and get her all set up.

"I'm so sorry," Jed told them as he closed his cell. "Something urgent about Owen Black, and I have to leave." His shoulders slumped. "And I had so many plans for us for these next few days," he told Mattie, his expression one of true disappointment.

"It's all right, Jed," Mattie said, clearly disappointed as well. "I was looking forward to our time together, too. But right now, this thing with Owen Black has to come first."

Reluctantly, Jed agreed. "But I'll definitely be in touch as soon as I know anything." He turned to Scotty. "Sorry about all this, Scotty. I'll drop you back at your place, and then be on my way."

Scotty gave Mattie a hug and started down the hall as she and Jed embraced. "Will you think about what I said?" he asked, smiling down at her. She nodded, and he kissed her cheek lightly.

Jed caught up with Scotty outside in the parking area. When they got in the car, Scotty said, "Well, did you tell her?"

"Yes; finally! I couldn't wait any longer."

"So, what'd she say?"

A sly grin filled Jed's face. "She didn't tell me to get lost!" He and Scotty then slapped each other a high five. "But it's just a little too soon after Gabe. And with all this mess about the estate...It's an awful situation."

"Sounds like Aunt Mattie just needs a little more time, Jed."

"I think so. But I'll wait. I'm very patient, you know. And someone like your aunt is so worth waiting for!"

Scotty nodded, grinning. "But I'd sure like to get my hands on Eva," he grumbled, "and wring her neck." He grew thoughtful. "I wonder where she is?"

The corner of Jed's mouth curved into the start of a smile, but Scotty was looking out the car window and didn't notice.

Back in her room, Mattie found it impossible to get Jed out of her mind. Sitting back in her chair and staring out her window, she went over his words again and again. Why hadn't she seen it coming? She recalled some of their earlier conversations, the tone of his voice, being number one on his case list; then, it all started to come together. Shaking her head as if to clear cobwebs, she reminded herself that it had only been a short time since Gabe had passed, after all—not even a year. It was just too soon to be thinking romantically about Jed or any other man, she scolded herself. How would that have made Gabe feel? The whole idea was totally absurd! *Why do I feel like a teenager all of a sudden? Jed's smile? His touch? The way he looks at me?* "Whew!" she sighed, rolling her eyes, resolution drifting out the window.

The sound of her phone ringing nearly jarred Mattie. She cleared her throat, tried to regain her composure and picked up the receiver. "Hello?" she said brightly but with a noticeable catch in her voice. She could've kicked herself.

"Mattie? Is that you? This is Marion." It was one of Mattie's neighbors from the condo development in Asheville. The two of them had enjoyed each other's company and would often get together while Gabe and Marion's husband, Gilbert, played golf.

"Marion! It's so great to hear from you. Is everything okay up your way?"

"Everything's fine. I've been busy with my daughter. She was here for the past few months and left just a couple days ago. I'm sorry I haven't called you before this, but we were trying to help her after her divorce. Well, you can imagine."

Mattie smiled. "Of course. And I wanted to call you, too, but in the sudden move here I lost my phone numbers and still haven't found them! And you know I'm not good at remembering numbers."

They laughed, and Marion asked how she was doing without Gabe. "It was so sudden, wasn't it, Mattie? And everything that happened afterwards with your estate and all; it was just awful."

"You're telling me. But I have someone" she cleared her throat again, "working on the estate, and hopefully, we'll get things resolved."

"That's good" Marion said. "Well, I thought we could do lunch some day. What if I come pick you up, and we'll go from there?"

"Sounds wonderful! But I couldn't tell you how to get here if I had to," Mattie said; "it's so far out in the boonies." Then she added, "Just head for the moon and take a left." They laughed again and Mattie told her, "I'll get directions from someone and get back to you."

"Oh, I'll just look you up on the Internet, Mattie. But I'll give you my cell number so you'll be sure to have it." Mattie wrote down the number and put it right next to her phone.

"Now why didn't I think of going to the Internet?" Mattie said. "I have a computer now, myself—a nice laptop. My nephew brought it over. Anyway, you'll have to give me your email address when we get together." They chirped away a few more minutes, making lunch plans, then said their good-byes. After hanging up, Mattie felt ten feet tall.

She went to her computer to check out Autumn Leaves on the internet. After several attempts, however, she came up with nothing. "Rats," she muttered, sagging; "I'll have to have Scotty help me. That boy knows more than he lets on.

It was late Saturday afternoon and Scotty showed up at Mattie's without phoning. It made her happy to think he felt comfortable enough to stay in touch the way he did. He was like a son to her and that felt good.

Propped at her computer, Scotty went from one file to another, scanning this, filling in that, while she watched. After making a few more entries, he chirped, "You're ready to roll, Aunt Mattie. You've got my email address and Jed's. Now here's how you take care of your mail." Then he had her go through all of it and send him a message.

"It worked!" she squealed. "Well, I'm just so proud of myself. Thanks for all your help, Scotty. I really appreciate it." Then she mentioned how she had tried to bring up the center on the internet and couldn't. So, Scotty searched for it —with no luck, either.

"What the hell?" he muttered. "It's gotta' be here." Then he showed her a map of the area where existing buildings were shown. He pointed out a farm, then a block with no name, then a nursery.

"That must be Jean's farm," Mattie said, pointing to the map. "She's a real nice lady who owns a dog. I've even sneaked...uh...brought the dog inside the center here."

Scotty glanced mischievously at her when she said that and snickered, then returned to the computer map. "Hmm.

This has me curious. I thought the center was privately owned. You'd think their name would show up. Oh, well; I'll check it out later."

"It is privately owned. By a Mr. Prescott. I met him several weeks ago when I...uh...well, when I sort of ran into him."

Scotty gave her a look of disbelief. "You sort of ran into him?" he teased. "What kind of trouble were you in?"

Mattie swatted him playfully, and that started a routine of hand slapping each other that had been going on for years, when one of them accused the other of being up to no good. She ended up giggling and hugging his neck.

After stretching his arms, Scotty stood, pulled out his car keys, and said, "Aunt Mattie, I better run. I'm picking up Lauren at seven, and I don't wanna' be late." His eyes lit up like a couple of fireworks when he said that. "Good luck with the email stuff," he told her.

"Good luck with your date," she came back, watching him hurry off. She thought about the two of them going out together. "'Picking her up at seven,'" she said aloud. "Has a nice ring to it." She stepped back inside her room. "Scotty and Lauren. Who would have thought?"

 10

Eva was smearing sun block on her arms and legs, while the warm breezes were dancing on Condado Beach. It had been several days since she'd seen Christine and the bodyguard. It was as if they'd up and disappeared. She gave a long sigh, lying back on a chaise and sipping Chardonnay, which she'd gone back to, since Christine wasn't there to impress.

"I must've done something wrong, or said something," Eva muttered to herself in anger. She flung the tube of lotion into the sand in a gesture of self-loathing. "Just when I thought things were going so good," she murmured, scowling. "Oh, what's the use?" With that, she stood and brushed some sand from the orange sequined bathing suit, tossed her beach bag over a shoulder and plodded back to her villa.

Heading inside the gate, she thought she heard her name being called. Looking around, she saw no one and continued on.

"Eva! Eva! It's Christine!" Eva stopped in her tracks. Heading her way with a look of concern was Eva's new friend. Christine began apologizing as she approached. "I'm so sorry, dear. We were called home to Key West. My mother became sick and we didn't know if she was going to make it. There wasn't time to let you know I'd be gone." Eva nearly dropped over when Christine embraced her warmly. "You do forgive me, don't you?"

Eva's expression rose to the level of near-arrogance. "Oh sure, Christine, of course. But how's your mother? Is she okay?" she asked, not really caring but feigning concern.

"Yes, she's much better now, thanks. The doctors think it was that flu virus that's been going around. With Mother's heart condition, they wondered if she'd make it." The women were strolling along chatting, with Christine's arm still around Eva. "But it looks like things are going better now. She's back home. I hired a nurse to be at her side twenty-four-seven. I insisted."

Eva laughed her silly laugh. "Those nurses can be expensive. I know; I had to have one for my stepmother," she lied.

They paused and Christine turned to her. "Really? What was the problem?"

"Oh, uh, well, she was getting...I don't know...senile, I guess, and we had to get her into a place. But before we moved her, she gave us all kinds of trouble. Arguing, fighting, temper tantrums. You wouldn't believe!" Eva said, shaking her head. "I actually felt sorry for the home nurse we hired to stay with her. I finally had to contact the lawyer and have everything put in my name."

Christine frowned sympathetically. "That must've been terribly difficult for you, Eva. You're a sweet girl, and it sounds like you've been through a lot." Eva looked away, smiling smugly to herself.

They stopped in front of Eva's place. "By the way," Christine said, "I'm having Sybil and Milford. You remember; the couple I introduced you to?" Eva nodded. "Anyway, we're getting together for cocktails tomorrow evening around six at my place." She smiled pleasantly at Eva. "And I'd like you to be there, too," she said, giving Eva's hand an affectionate squeeze. "That is, if you don't already have plans?"

"No, no," Eva was quick to respond. "No, I'm free tomorrow evening." Christine gave her another hug, told her how to get to her condo and they said their good-byes.

Eva had self-importance written all over her face. "I knew it," she muttered, smiling as she entered her villa. "I'll be a part of that little circle before tomorrow night is over!"

Eva was wearing a grey blouse, black jeans, and thong sandals when she arrived at Christine's the next evening. She had stopped at the beach bar and picked up some of the prepared Margarita mix she knew her friend enjoyed.

"Eva, you shouldn't have!" Christine said, greeting her at the door with a hug and setting the bottle aside. Christine looked as if she'd just stepped out of a magazine, with her pretty blond hair, a turquoise tank top studded with white pearls, white linen cropped pants, and white heels—and, of course, that stunning bracelet. "Come in," she told Eva enthusiastically.

"Sybil and Milford, look who's here!" she called to the others. Wearing casual but chic beachwear, they smiled and greeted Eva warmly, with Milford standing until Eva took a seat. The bodyguard Jason, who stood off to one side, nodded at her.

Sitting on the off-white circular sofa scattered with bright coral and aqua pillows, Eva appeared wide-eyed as she took in her surroundings. The condo, open and spacious with towering ceilings, pillars and walls of windows overlooking the water, gave off a classy beach house air. Hanging on the shell-colored walls, the contemporary works of art alone must have been worth thousands!

Jason took care of everyone's drinks, while Christine set out some avocados with warm butter and crackers. Then he took a seat off to one side near the white marble fireplace. The others chatted amiably for some time about nothing in particular and things in general.

"By the way, Christine," Milford said, sitting back relaxed with his drink, then crossing his feet out in front of him. "How's that investment of yours coming along?"

"Ohh, Milford," she crooned, wide-eyed then; "I can't believe how well it's doing! I'm just happy you told me about it."

Sybil spoke up. "Christine, dear, we wanted you to get in on this discovery before it reaches the news media. And you know what'll happen then." She looked at Milford with her thumb pointing down.

Having no knowledge of stocks or of the investing world, Eva sat back out of the conversation, guzzling her drink but taking everything in.

"But how about you?" Christine asked Milford; "are your shares paying off?"

He chuckled, and then gave a whistle. "Ten thousand in two months, and going up. I'd call that paying off!"

"I'll say!" Christine said, laughing, while Eva's eyes had grown twice their size on hearing about his good fortune. Sipping more of her drink, Christine lowered her voice. "Who would have thought a simple gemstone could possess such paying power!" Then she turned to Eva and began apologizing, while patting her hand. "Oh, Eva, I am so sorry. We get on these investment kicks and forget anyone else is around." She set her drink down and glanced back at Eva. "Unless you're into investments?"

Eva shook her head. "Oh, no I'm not really much for stocks and that sort of thing," she said, finishing her drink.

"But would you be?" It was Milford.

"Uh, well, I-I really don't know much about things like that."

He set his drink down, and then leaned forward facing her. "This deal is so fabulous, Eva, there's no way it could go wrong."

"And, Eva," Christine said warmly, "we've gotten to be good friends. If you'd like to think about going in with us, we'd be glad to help you."

"You would?"

In unison, they all agreed. "Eva," the motherly Sybil said, "if we thought there was any trouble—any trouble at all—with this whole investment thing, we would have said no thanks right from the start, believe me."

Jason had poured more drinks for them, and Eva gulped down much of hers right away. "I must admit," she said, as though trying to sound more business savvy, "I am curious. But what is this gemstone you're talking about?"

"Ahh," Milford spoke up, finishing his drink. "There's a mine just recently discovered, somewhere out in the western states; Colorado, I think. Anyway, they've just found an abundant supply of one of the most beautiful gems in the world: Angelite. It's sparkly; not as strong as diamonds; stronger than zirconium; and absolutely beautiful—like an angel. There must be hundreds of miles of caves and old mines that are just now being discovered!" He watched Christine get up off the sofa and head for a bedroom down the hall. "Christine will show you," he said, his eyes lighting up.

When Christine returned, she was carrying a small sack with a drawstring and emptied it carefully onto the coffee table. She appeared close to tears while she showed the sparkling little jewels to Eva. "Look, Eva," she said, her voice close to a whisper. "Aren't they gorgeous?!"

"I have to admit," Eva said, now completely wrapped up in the gemstone thing, "they are beautiful."

"We can get you in on the deal, if you want, Eva," Milford said. "But only if you're interested. I'm not trying to push it or anything like that. After all, I'm planning to invest even more, myself!"

Eva squirmed a little and asked, "How much would I have to invest?"

"Oh, not that much, Eva," Sybil said. She gave a shrug. "Five hundred or so."

Eva perked up then. "Only five hundred dollars?"

The room was in complete silence as the others stared at her. Finally, Milford gave a hearty laugh. "Five hundred dollars!" He laughed again. "Eva, you have quite a sense of humor!" He chuckled again, while the women smiled. Then he said, "Five hundred thousand, Eva!"

Eva let out a gasp and chugged more of her drink. By that time, she was beginning to feel the effects of the alcohol, but could have cared less. "I'll have to think about this," she said, her words becoming slurred. "Besides, I didn't bring my checkbook," she said, adding her silly laugh.

"Eva, it's all right," Christine said warmly. "If you'd like, you can bring me the money tomorrow and I'll make sure it gets to Austin. He's our broker here," she explained. "How's that sound?"

"Well, I—" Eva was interrupted by Milford. "But, Christine," he said, "what about the cut-off date?"

Christine sucked in a gasp and flopped back on the sofa. "Oh, no." She looked at Eva as though she were about to break down. "Oh, Eva, dear; the cutoff date to enroll in the investment is midnight tonight!" And she let out a little moan. "But if you could still get me the money," she said, excitedly, "I'll just call Austin, and tell him you're in on the deal, and he'll have the paperwork ready, and we could pick it up tomorrow—that is, if you're okay with all of this. Oh, Eva, the money we're all going to make!" Then she looked Eva straight in the eye and said, "You're not afraid, are you Eva?"

That was all it took. Anyone who knew Eva would know she had to save face in front of her wheeler-dealer friends. Between that and the drinks, Eva agreed. "I'll get you the money, right now," she told Christine firmly.

"And don't worry, Eva," Milford assured her, "you'll probably get a return on it two times over." Of course, Sybil heartily agreed.

"Wow, this is so exciting!" Eva chirped. She got up to head back to her villa, but her footing was a bit unstable from the drinking. So, Milford offered to accompany her, jokingly claiming that he wanted to protect her from some of the "predators" who might try to come on to her—since she was "such an attractive young lady," he said, loud enough for the others to hear.

Giddy then, Eva threw her arms around all three of them. "I've never felt so wonderful and so cared about in my life!" she exclaimed, while the others returned her hugs.

"We'll be back shortly," Milford said, and he and Eva left with him at Eva's elbow to make certain she didn't take a fall.

Returning to Christine's condo a short time later with Eva and her checkbook, Milford led her to the sofa and helped her get seated. Sybil was in the process of writing another investment check for Christine, and Christine was still fingering the "Angelite" gems.

"This is my special checkbook," Eva told everyone happily, while writing the check. She had either forgotten or didn't care that the check would eat up much of the money from the estate. Then she began fanning herself. "Is it warm in here?"

"Oh, you're probably just excited about everything," Milford assured her, drawing out a checkbook and proceeding to write his own check for Christine. "Incidentally, Eva," he said, "er, if you don't mind me asking, just how did you come into your money?"

Eva paused and looked puzzled, while Jason brought another cocktail, which she began chugging down hurriedly.

Christine answered for her. "Eva told me she had to put her father's house and everything he owned into her name. All of which was done legally, Milford, not *quite* like the way *you* came into *your* money," she reminded him, giving him a cunning little smile.

"Now, now, Christine. We can't be giving Eva the wrong impression. She's too much a lady to be hearing about things that, well, might be considered 'unscrupulous'."

Sybil swatted his arm playfully and said, "Milford, you know that last transaction you got involved in with the soybeans was far from legal."

"But who's going to know?" He glanced at Eva. "...besides Eva? And you wouldn't say anything, would you Eva?"

With the conversation taking a tell-all and slightly "unethical" turn, Eva, half-sloshed, opened up. "You'll never believe how I got my money, how I really got it," she said. All eyes were on her. "That story I told you wasn't completely true, Christine."

Christine looked puzzled. "About your stepmother, you mean?"

"Yeah," Eva said, giggling and practically drooling over what she was about to reveal. "It didn't happen quite that way."

"Eva, you sly little fox!" Christine said, grinning in admiration. She turned to the others. "This girl's been holding out on us." Christine leaned forward then, her hand resting on her chin, facing Eva. "You're getting more and more intriguing by the minute, Eva. Go on, please! I have to hear this!"

Mary A. Berger

Late one morning Mattie's phone rang. It was one of the "Agents" from her rally. "Mattie, I just spotted Reemes in his office. Let's go!"

Mattie dropped everything, snatched up a folder that held the signed petition and nearly ran down the hall to meet the others at Reemes' office. Five of the Agents were there and, of course, they looked to Mattie to start the ball rolling.

Without hesitating, she stepped right up to the plate. Knocking politely on Mr. Reemes' door, she said, "Excuse me, Mr. Reemes, we have some things we'd like to discuss with you." And without waiting for his okay, she stepped into his office, waving the others in.

He sat back frowning. "You, again, Mrs. Morgan? What is this? What's going on here?"

"As I said, we all have some things we feel are important that we want to talk to you about."

"But you can't just come barging in here, especially without an appointment. Now, let me look at my calendar." And Reemes began thumbing through the pages on his desk calendar. "I have a few minutes right before Christmas," he told them sarcastically.

They were all shaking their heads and Clint spoke up. "Not soon enough, Mr. Reemes. We think today would be good. Right now, in fact." And he turned to Mattie, who was holding the folder and said, "Mattie; wasn't there something about a petition?"

"Right here," she said, shoving the makeshift document under Mr. Reemes' nose.

The others grew more courageous and backed up Mattie and Clint by putting in their two cents' worth. Being surrounded by so many of them, Reemes began fidgeting, and then said with an impatient sigh, "All right, all right; let's see what you people have to say here." Mr. Reemes ran over the petition, murmuring to himself parts of their requests. Then he tossed the document onto his desk. "I'll see what I can do," he told them. "But I'm making no promises."

"When will we know if anything's being done?" Mattie asked.

Still impatient, he waved his hand back and forth and said, "Oh, some day."

"When?"

The others stood staring at him awaiting his reply. "Okay, okay—soon."

They all thanked him, and Mattie added, "We'll all be watching for changes—*soon*." And the little band of renegades turned and left his office.

Walking silently together until they turned a corner out of Reemes' sight, Mattie spouted, "See, what'd I tell you? It took all of us together to make him listen!" They exchanged high fives and the guys let out whistles. "Hell's bells," Mattie said. "If I'd been in there alone with him, well, let's just say I might have a new address by now!"

"We can't let that happen," someone called out. Before they all split up, Mattie assured them she'd keep on top of the progress, if any, and so should the rest of them.

Suddenly, Clint sagged. "Uh-oh," he said. "Mattie, I just happened to think: we left the signed petition with Mr.

Reemes. Now we don't have the paper or any ammunition to back us up! I think we should go back and—"

"Relax, Clint," Mattie scoffed. "That was just a copy. I ran our original petition through my copier. Come on, people, do you think I would have trusted Reemes with the original? It's right here." And she patted the folder, while more cheers went up. "And here are copies for each of you," she said, reaching inside the folder and handing out copies to the others. "Just so we all keep on top of things." She held her head proudly, then sounding most businesslike, she said, "Now let's not forget to keep the Partners informed about all this."

Mattie could sense a change in the air. She was uplifted by the progress she was making in getting her fellow inmates stirred up. That was a start; and it felt good.

Another concern of hers was that greenhouse area. Though it was late for planting, Mattie had sent away for a seed catalog. After it arrived, she ordered a few zinnias, pansies, and impatiens, and invested in several inexpensive planter pods for getting the seeds started. Being that it was the middle of summer, she didn't expect too much from any of the little plantings; yet, if she could get them growing out at the greenhouse, perhaps it would at least begin to show the early, yet fragile beginnings of something more substantial.

Now if she could round up some of the others to give her a hand.

She managed to get Lillian, Kathy and a couple of others to agree to help her. They strolled out toward the "back forty" as Mattie liked to call it, and saw Hank at the old shed, still working on the riding lawn mower.

"Mornin' ladies," he greeted them, and Mattie introduced all of them.

"Say, Hank, you wouldn't by any chance have some old rope and stakes we could borrow, would you?" asked Mattie. He removed his Braves cap and scratched his head. "Well, Miss Mattie, let me have a look 'round here."

While he moved some old boxes and rearranged a few tools, the women chatted among themselves.

"This guy's a hoot," Mattie told them, grinning. "He has one funny line after another."

Actually, Hank did manage to find some rope, not much, but enough so the ends could be tied together making the sections longer, and then he came up with some old sticks that had been used as fencing. "What in Tar Nation y'all want this for?" he asked.

"We're going to build a shrine to Autumn Leaves," Mattie answered jokingly. "Actually, we want to put some plants and things out where the old greenhouse used to be, and we want to cordon off the area to try to make it look like something's happening there."

Hank nodded. He couldn't resist the audience he had then, and started in on one of his stories. "Say, ladies, I was thinkin', y'all know how these days everyone's carrying around a cell phone, like a status symbol, either clipped on their belt or purse? I can't afford one so I'm wearing my garage door opener."

Naturally, the women laughed, so he threw out another one.

"Y'know, I see more people reading the Bible as they get older. Then it dawned on me, they're cramming for their finals."

"Hank," Kathy said, laughing, "you should come inside some day and tell jokes for all of the people. We sure could use that!"

Her remark resonated with Mattie and she squealed, "Kathy, that's a wonderful idea!" She turned to Hank. "What do you say, Hank? Would you do that for us?"

Hank waved them off with a "Shucks, I'm not that good." But Mattie could see him beaming.

"But would you just think about it?" she asked him. "You'd make a lot of us happy." "Oh, I dunno," he said, chuckling to himself. "I might."

One of the women said, "He's a man. He just wants us to beg him a little."

At the greenhouse, the women looked around and found some old cinder blocks, stood them upright and propped the plants on them. And Mattie found a good-sized rock to pound the sticks in with. Then they tied the rope pieces together and wrapped them around the sticks, encircling the little plantings, which Mattie had watered before leaving the center.

"Not bad," Mattie said, standing back admiring the crude but heartfelt project.

"Yeah, now let's hope the critters don't get to them," said Lillian. "I have to admit, Mattie, it does look nice." The others agreed, and smiled proudly.

After they'd finished up and returned to the center, Hank strolled out to the greenhouse area and looked around. Removing his cap, he scratched his head and said to himself, "Well, I'll be. Them women are serious. Maybe I can give 'em a hand."

A few days later, toting a water jug in one hand, Mattie tried to talk Clare into taking a stroll with her, "to see what we've done out at the greenhouse," she said; "pleeeze, Clare?"

After more begging on Mattie's part and complaining on Clare's part, Clare finally gave in. "Is this project going to be written up in the Guinness Book of Wanna-be Gardeners?" she asked, in her usual brash way.

"I'll have you written up for being the world's worst whiner," Mattie came back, and they both giggled and continued on with an arm around each other's waist.

When they arrived, Clare stopped in her tracks. "Wow, Matts; it really does look nice! You girls did all this?"

Mattie looked around in disbelief. Where the cinder blocks had stood were pedestals of drain tiles, painted in colorful tones. Earthenware pots, sitting on top of the drain tiles and holding Mattie's plants, replaced the little plastic flower containers. Beyond them, in place of the old ropes and sticks, were short columns of deck timbers, draped with real pier rope and attached to each other by metal rings. All were arranged in a semi-circle around the entire area, which had been weeded and raked, and in the middle of which now sat a small wooden patio bench.

Mattie didn't know what to say. She turned to Clare. "Clare, it didn't look this nice when we left the other day. This is amazing! I wonder who or how"

"Don't look a garden gift-horse in the ass," Clare told her. "Just enjoy."

Back in the center, Mattie and Clare were about to stop in the dining room at the soda machine, when Mr. Reemes caught up with them. "Here we go again," Mattie muttered under her breath.

"Mrs. Morgan!" He sounded as though he were ready to explode. "Were you or were you not out back at the old greenhouse area?"

"Of course."

"Wha...what? Then you admit it?"

"We were both there," Clare chimed in, stepping closer to him and getting in his face. "What about it?"

"For your information, ladies, there happens to be a No Trespassing sign posted. Were you aware of that?"

"Oh, that," Mattie said with a wave of her hand. "I don't pay attention to things like that." She gave a shrug. "I thought some kids were probably horsing around and put it up to scare us. Besides, sir, who would deny the people here the opportunity to grow flowers and learn about plants and gardening?" He started to respond but she cut him off. "I'd say a project like that would be a feather in your cap; wouldn't you agree, Clare?"

"Feather in your cap," Clare echoed.

Reemes folded his arms, gave an impatient sigh, when Hank came by toting a ladder. "Hello, ladies," he said, tipping his cap, and turning to Jim Reemes. "Mr. Reemes."

Mattie saw the opportunity and jumped on it. "Oh, Hank, do you know anything about the greenhouse, I mean, who fixed it up for us?"

Hank looked down, smiling to himself. "It was you!" Mattie squealed gratefully. "Thank you, thank you! Mr. Reemes, you should go out there and see for yourself. Hank, here, helped us dress it up and now it's so pretty! I mean, really!"

Reemes was caught again and he knew it, and didn't like it one bit. "All right, all right," he said, relenting, while Hank strolled off, grinning. "But you'll have to sign a waver each time any one of you sets foot out there. Understood?" he barked before walking away.

"No problem," Mattie called sweetly after him. Under her breath, she turned back to Clare and grumbled, "I'd like to yank him by his family jewels and—"

"Oh, Mattie, you're such a little 'hottie,'" Clare said, keeping a straight face.

Then Mattie remembered wanting to speak with Harold Bates. "Oh, Clare, let's go talk to Mr. Bates and see if we can get a program or something lined up with Hank. Wha'd'you say? Want to come with me?"

"Why not?" Clare said, and then she stopped short. "Oh, I almost forgot. I told my cousin I'd call her back. You know; the one who's so bitchy every time she calls me?" Clare gave a sigh. "I better go do that or I'll really be on her you-know-what list."

"Sounds like you already are," Mattie said, while Clare strolled away, chuckling.

So Mattie headed off by herself and found Harold Bates getting ready to leave for the day. "Mr. Bates?" she called to him. "Do you have a minute?"

"Hi, Mrs. Morgan. What's on your mind?"

"I've found out that Hank, our yard man, has a way with telling jokes and stories. Do you suppose we could get him to do a program for us? You know, like a stand-up comic?"

"He's that funny?"

"Yes. And having someone like him entertain us would give everyone a lift, don't you agree?"

"Sounds good to me. Why don't you see if you can line him up?"

"You want me to do that?"

"Of course," he said, grinning. "You're the git-'er-done girl, aren't you?"

"Yeah, I guess I am," Mattie said, beaming before heading back to her room.

Along the way, she felt a sudden urge to use the bathroom. Since she was so close to the public restroom, she turned and opened the door. Stepping inside, she stopped in her tracks.

"Whoa!" she murmured. She wasn't in the ladies room. Glancing around, it dawned on her she had opened the wrong door. "Good grief!" she whispered. "It's the room where they keep the trouble makers locked up!" Reemes or someone had apparently forgotten to lock the door. Instinct told her to turn right around and leave. But curiosity won out.

Before her, a computer was lit up, with a screen saver roaming; a printer set up next to it; and a small tray, which held copies of some sort of certificate. Looking closer, she could see clearly what it was. Certificates of approval for Autumn Leaves, with the state name and dates on them for the next three years! "What is this?" she muttered.

Glancing around to make sure no one had seen her come in, she went to the computer. Knowing one tap on a key would bring the screen to life, she did just that. Immediately, Mattie stood staring at the current Autumn Leaves budget page, her mouth falling open in amazement. The screen showed a record of the center's expenses, income, travel plans for Reemes and

Prescott, and, what looked to Mattie like a little "creative accounting" with income figures being filtered into their travel budget!

"Ka-ching!" Mattie spouted, then, "Yikes, I've got to get out of here!" Hastily, she tapped the "save" button on the keyboard to return the screen saver and casually walked back out in the hall, closing the door quietly behind her. "Whew!" she breathed, swallowing hard, and then she headed straight for her room.

Pacing the floor there, Mattie ran through everything. The computer and schedules. The printed certificates.

What did it all mean? She sat in her chair, sorting things out. Okay, she told herself, the computer showed the current Autumn Leaves budget. Fine, but what about the figures showing funds being directed into Reemes' and Prescott's travel accounts?

Maybe it was Mattie's banking background or secretarial training, maybe it was just the orderly way her mind worked. She got out her little note pad and began making notes of everything she'd seen, even the copies of the certificates of approval, not fully realizing the impact of it all.

After much thought, Mattie put the kettle on for tea and made herself some soup. She decided to remain quiet about her discovery—at least for now. She thought about emailing Jed with the information, but something held her back. She was hesitant about sending things like that into cyber space. She decided against it. Should she tell Mr. Bates? she wondered. *Yes.* That's exactly what she would do. First thing tomorrow.

The next day, Mattie put on her purple jogging suit and "tennies," ran through her stretches, and then had a light breakfast. She purposely waited until around ten o'clock in order to give Mr. Bates time to take care of whatever his early morning office routine might entail. Then she headed down the hall.

As luck would have it, Mr. Bates was nowhere around. Sagging, Mattie strolled about the halls, searching for him.

Lauren came by and they talked for a few minutes. "Let's go out on the porch," Lauren said. "We haven't had a chat for a while."

Though Mattie wanted desperately to see Mr. Bates, she had grown so fond of Lauren, she couldn't resist her offer, and the two of them went outdoors.

"How have you been, Mrs. Morgan?" Lauren asked as they sat in the porch chairs.

"Oh, Lauren, I'm just trying to stay busy." Mattie remembered the greenhouse. "You should take a walk some day and wander out to where the old greenhouse was," she told Lauren. Then she filled her in on what had happened out there, and how Hank had helped the women.

"I'll do that!" Lauren said enthusiastically. Then she said, "Uh, Mrs. Morgan . . . y'all know I'm seeing your nephew?" Her bright brown eyes shone even brighter when she said that.

"Why, yes; Scotty told me you two were dating. He's such a nice guy, Lauren."

"I'll say! I've never had more fun with anyone in my life. We went to a NASCAR race the other night. It was so exciting!" It didn't take much to show Mattie how Lauren felt.

She looked at her young friend and with a crafty smile, said, "You kinda' like my nephew, don't you?"

Lauren smiled back. "Yeah...I do like him a lot."

"Oh, that's nice." Mattie reached over and patted her hand. "Because I'm pretty sure he feels the same about you." Her comment drew an even bigger smile from Lauren, whose cheeks colored a little.

Changing the subject then, Mattie asked, "Lauren, what's the problem with Mr. Reemes? He's always on the warpath."

Lauren grew serious. "I know." With a shrug, she added, "I'm just waiting for uh, well, I can't talk about it yet." She lowered her voice and looked straight at Mattie. "I don't trust

Mr. Reemes or Mr. Prescott."

"Well, if you don't trust them, how can the rest of us?"

"I don't know how to answer that. I'm just hoping something will..." she paused, and then looked away.

It was obvious that Lauren knew something and couldn't talk, so Mattie didn't press her.

While they were sitting together enjoying the sunshine, they noticed someone approaching from the back yard. It was Bernard. Lauren called to him and he waved to them. In so doing, he tilted his head back and a small branch from the big lilac bush caught his toupee, snatching it right off his head! The women both sucked in a gasp. Strangely, Bernard seemed unaware that his hairpiece was even gone.

"Should we tell him?" Mattie whispered, trying to keep a straight face.

"I don't know," Lauren squealed under her breath.

The unsuspecting, bald-as-a-baby Bernard came right over to the porch flashing his silly I-know-you-want-me grin and proceeded to talk to them in his usual suggestive way.

"Would one of you lovely ladies care to join me in my room for a little tip of the grape?" he asked, while lifting an eyebrow suggestively.

Meanwhile, behind his back, a breeze had loosened the toupee, which was blowing merrily across the yard. At that moment, the puppy, Scooter, happened by with Jean, and seeing the hairpiece, the dog began chasing after it as though it were a plaything. Each time he'd make a lunge for it the breeze would lift it up and carry it further, just out of his reach.

Tail wagging, the romping Scooter was having a great time, especially when he finally caught up with the wig and shook it like a rag doll.

While watching all this going on behind Bernard's back, Mattie's and Lauren could barely contain themselves. Finally, Jean managed to snatch up the toupee. She came right over to the porch. "Does this belong to anyone here?" she asked.

When Bernard saw his toupee, his hands flew to his head. His eyes bugged out and he almost hyperventilated. "Oh, Gawd!" he cried out. "My hair!" And he patted the snarled toupee lopsided onto his head. Nearly in tears, he kept saying, "Oh, no! Now everybody will know I'm bald! Oh, no!"

Jean stepped right up. "I'm so sorry," she said, getting hold of Scooter's collar; "my dog gets a little rambunctious sometimes. But, sir," she said, looking straight at Bernard. "I think y'all look much more handsome without that thing."

Bernard was speechless for a moment. Finally, he said, "You do? Really?"

"Absolutely. Don't you ladies agree?" Mattie and Lauren both nodded with straight faces.

"Really?" Bernard repeated, and his smile returned but seemed more genuine. "Is that a fact?" With that, he took off the matted, tangled hairpiece and stood a little taller and with a bit more confidence, Mattie thought, watching him stroll away.

"Thanks, Jean!" Mattie and Lauren both said. "I thought we were headed for a male-menopausal crisis!" Mattie chirped.

"I could hardly keep a straight face!" Lauren said. And she told Jean what had happened with the branch and

Bernard's toupee. "That rug looked awful, anyway! I'm kinda' glad the dog got hold of it."

Jean chuckled, and said she was just on her way back home and had to get going. The women thanked her again for the "good time" and both went back inside. Between the visit with Lauren and the toupee escapade, Mattie had nearly forgotten about seeing Mr. Bates. Luckily, she ran right into him as soon as she stepped inside.

"Mr. Bates, I need to talk to you," she called to him, after saying good-bye to Lauren.

"Sure thing. What can I do for you?"

"We need to go into your office," she told him.

Once inside, he could see Mattie's concern and closed his door. "What is it, Mrs. Morgan?"

Mattie sat back, took a deep breath, and told him about what she'd discovered in the room that was usually locked.

"I can't believe this," he said, looking mystified. "You're sure about everything you saw?"

"Of course." And she drew out her little notepad with the things she'd seen jotted down, "just so I didn't forget anything." She looked at him questioningly. "But what about you? Haven't you ever been in there or seen the computer?"

He gave a snort. "No way. That room's been padlocked for over a year—ever since I've been here." With a shrug, he went on. "I just figured there were old records or things of value in it that Reemes or Prescott didn't want anyone to get their hands on, you know, things they were protecting."

"They were protecting their rear ends," she said emphatically. "So what are you going to do now?"

Mr. Bates rubbed his chin thoughtfully. "I'm not sure. Let me think about this." After thanking her profoundly, he said with concern, "I'd stay out of that room if I were you."

"You don't have to tell me twice," she said, swallowing hard.

Mary A. Berger

 12

It was the day of Mattie's lunch date with Marion, who phoned to make sure their plans were still on.

"Oh, of course, Marion. I am so looking forward to seeing you again," Mattie told her enthusiastically. "And you know how to get here?"

Marion snickered. "Well, yes; but I couldn't find it on the internet, so I just asked around. I'm sure there'll be no problem. We'll try a new place not too far from where you are, okay?"

"I'm glad you know your way. I'd probably drive off the edge of the earth trying to find things around here, if it were up to me."

"Well, I'll be there in about an hour, all right?"

Of course, Mattie agreed and said she'd see her then.

The restaurant Marion had chosen turned out to be a lovely tearoom, perfect for their get-together. The sound of classical music greeted them as they entered the double French doors. White sheers hung at the windows topped with floral cornices, and a white linen tablecloth was draped over each table. Colorful cloth napkins dressed up each setting, while vases filled with summer pansies added to the ambiance.

"This is beautiful!" Mattie chirped, and Marion had to agree.

"Let's hope the food's as nice as the atmosphere," she said.

They were seated in a private corner booth, then a smiling waitress dressed in a long skirt and peasant top came by and took their orders. Mattie asked for a luncheon salad plate with an assortment of salads, while Marion wanted a spinach quiche, and they both ordered hot tea.

"Marion, I hate to admit this but I've completely lost my orientation around this area. Not being able to get out and about can really throw you. So where are we, say, in relation to Asheville, or Greenville, or Charlotte?"

"I know what you mean!" Marion said. "I almost lost my way out to your place. I can't imagine why it's so far from everything. Anyway, we're sort of in the middle between Asheville and Franklin and Hendersonville."

"That narrows it down," Mattie said grinning, then with a shrug she added, "as long as we're still in the United States."

The women chatted on like old friends, even though it had been months since they'd seen each other, and soon the waitress brought their food. "And what about your daughter?" Mattie asked, stirring her tea; "how are things going with her?"

"It's hard. But she's going back to college, so I think that will help." Mattie nodded in agreement and Marion changed the subject. "Mattie, tell me how are you doing there at the center? I mean how are you really doing?"

"Oh, I get by," Mattie said, digging into one of her salads. "It's easier than it was at first, though."

"I can imagine."

"The people who run the place are sharks, however. I think they use our rent money to finance their cruise vacations and golf outings."

Marion frowned. "Why, that's terrible. Can't you do something about it?"

"We're trying."

Eventually, the subject of Mattie's case came up. "Jed Mitchell's been working on it, and what a help he's been!" Mattie told her. "In fact, I don't know what I'd do without him."

Marion looked thoughtful. "I think I remember him from being at Gabe's funeral. Nice looking man. Is he a good man?"

"Oh, yes! The best!" And Mattie stopped eating momentarily, gazing into space, with her fork dangling in midair.

Marion picked up on it and with eyes shining asked teasingly, "Mattie; is there something you're not telling me?"

"You mean about Jed?"

"Yeah. I'm getting the feeling there's more to him than being a good lawyer."

"Oh, he's a terrific a lawyer. Everyone admires and respects him," Mattie said.

"And you?"

Mattie turned and looked into her friend's eyes. "As I said, Marion, I can't help but appreciate all he..." Her voice grew weak.

Marion smiled knowingly. "You have feelings for him, don't you Mattie?" Mattie could only look at her, and Marion added, "Just don't get those feelings confused with obligation towards him, after all the help he's given you."

"Oh, Marion, he's so good to me," Mattie said, eyes glowing. "And I know he likes me. And I feel like a teenager when we're together."

"Uh-oh," Marion said. "That doesn't sound like 'obligation' to me." And the two of them giggled, while Marion squeezed Mattie's arm affectionately.

Mattie grew serious then. "But Marion, it hasn't even been a year since Gabe died. It's too soon to be thinking about another man; isn't it?"

Marion sipped some of her tea. "Mattie, would you believe Gil and I got married less than three months after my first husband passed away?" Mattie stared in disbelief. "But we were both so lonely. Right now, I can't imagine that part of my life without Gil. If we had listened to family and friends, telling us it was too soon, we'd probably still be dating!"

"Really?" asked Mattie, all ears.

"Life is for the living, Mattie. You know that better than anyone. You fulfilled your marriage pledge: 'til death do we part. Gabe is gone. Your life with him was wonderful, I know. But you're still young and pretty; you have to put Gabe in the past and think about now." She reached over and patted Mattie's hand. "And you deserve to be happy."

Mattie took to heart everything her friend said. Being older, Marion had Mattie's complete respect and admiration.

"It's been wonderful talking to you," Mattie said, sipping her tea.

After the pleasant outing, the women headed back to Autumn Leaves and promised to get together again soon. And Mattie felt as if she'd gained a new lease on life.

13

Sitting in his box-like office, Harold Bates answered the beeping of his phone. "Harold Bates speaking."

"Hello, Mr. Bates. This is Kerrie Kane calling from TV. station WYMT. We saw the piece in your local newspaper a few months ago about the puppy?"

Mr. Bates frowned momentarily, and then remembered the article that told how Mattie had brought in the dog for Fae Munn. "Yes, yes, of course! What can I do for you, Ms. Kane?"

"I'm sorry it's taken me so long to get in touch with you, but we all thought the newspaper story was so neat that we'd like to do a similar piece for our community segment on the six o'clock news. Would it be all right if we brought our cameras and did the spot right there at the center?"

Mr. Bates inhaled deeply. "*Here?* You want to film it *here?*"

"If that's okay with you. We thought an on-site report would give it a more human touch. Dogs, especially dogs helping people, generate tons of appeal for our viewers. We're hoping we can film the dog, and maybe the women involved. We'd like to come out on the fifteenth, that's next Tuesday afternoon. So, do I have your permission then?"

"Absolutely! Thank you; and you will call before you come, just to be in touch?"

"Oh, yes; we'll be in touch. We'll need to find our way out there. Thanks!"

When Bates hung up, he noticed Jim Reemes at the water cooler. "Hey, Jim, you'll never guess who that was," he called out enthusiastically. After relaying the news to Reemes, who could barely hide his panic, Harold Bates went to find Lauren to ask if she'd help him round up some of the others to get things shaped up, at least as much as they could, for the cameras. They even lined up Hank to touch up and re-hang the Autumn Leaves sign out front.

Meanwhile, Jim Reemes stood dabbing a handkerchief at the thousand beads of sweat on his forehead. Then his eyes grew big as baseballs. "Oh, Lord—*Mrs. Morgan!*" he cried. "If she gets involved in this—" (and he knew from previous experience, somehow she would). "The fifteenth...hmm. We'll see about that." He stood staring out the lobby window, and then suddenly took off down the hall for Mattie's.

Approaching her room, he stopped, took a deep breath, and squared his shoulders. Then he tapped on her door. "Hope the little witch is here," he said to himself.

"Come in," Mattie called without looking up from her computer.

"Uh, Mrs. Morgan. It's nice to see you."

Mattie swung around in her chair, stunned. "Mr. Reemes, I haven't done anything wrong. Really!"

"No, no; nothing like that," he said with a tight laugh. "I've been thinking, er, may I sit down?" he asked, pulling out a chair.

Mattie squinted suspiciously and said slowly, "Yes-s-s."

"Thank you."

Mattie saw his discomfort. "Mr. Reemes, we both know there's no love lost between us. Get to the point."

For a split second, his eyes narrowed, but then he forced a smile. "What I'm here about is: there's a conference coming up in Winston-Salem—Old Salem, actually. It's for a bunch of hotel owners and people who run places like Autumn Leaves." He eyed her cautiously.

"Go on," she said, also cautiously.

"Well, what they do is discuss ways to improve our surroundings and business practices. They're asking for representatives to attend. I can't go this year; Mr. Prescott is away, and Mr. Bates has other plans. So my question to you is this, would you consider being our representative?"

Mattie laughed out loud. "You mean you'd send me out to a conference, knowing I'd spout off like a geyser about Autumn Leaves?"

"Maybe that's what they need to hear. Personally," he said, turning away to stifle a sudden cough, "I believe you'd make a good rep. You'd have to stay overnight, but there's a wonderful inn in Old Salem where we'd put you up—at our expense, of course." He went on, but the catch in his throat was there again. "I'll...cough...cough...I'll even loan you my car so you'll have your own transportation."

"Oh, that's not necessary," she said hastily. "My nephew would be able to run me over there." By now, Mattie really smelled a rat, but something told her to go along with it, out of curiosity if nothing else. "But I'll think about the conference. When is it?"

Reemes acted as if he was trying not to look nervous. "Uh, next Tuesday, the fifteenth." Mattie checked her computer calendar.

"I think I can manage that," she said, still somewhat cautious.

"Here's some paperwork and directions you can look over," he said, handing them to her. Then he almost sprang from the chair. "Thank you. Thank you very much, Mrs. Morgan."

Without another word, he hurried from her room. *Did he have a sudden change of heart?* she wondered. No way; there was something else going on. *Maybe he's afraid of me*, she thought with a chuckle. However, thinking back to that day in his office when the two of them had had a showdown of sorts, she felt her skin crawl all over again with goose bumps.

Returning to her computer, where she was in the middle of a note to Jed, telling him how much she loved hearing from him nearly every day, she noticed an incoming email from Scotty. He told her a little about his date with Lauren, how they'd both had a great time and were going out to dinner and a ball game in a few days. Mattie smiled reading it, then went back, and finished her note to Jed.

After a while, she heated some water in the teakettle and made tea. She had just taken it to her little table, when she heard another tap at her door. "Mrs. Morgan? Feel like some company for a few minutes?"

"Mr. Bates! Come in, come in. Would you like some peppermint tea?"

He nodded, and she poured more hot water and made a cup for him. They began an easy conversation and it seemed to Mattie the longer they chatted, the more trusting of him she began to feel.

"Mr. Bates, I—"

"Harold. Call me Harold. Please."

She smiled. "Okay, 'Harold'. I've been wondering, why is it you stay here in this dump?

"Mrs. Morgan, I—"

"It's Mattalie. But call me Mattie, please."

He chuckled lightly and the two of them instinctively reached out and shook hands. "All right, 'Mattie'. You see, I love doing what I do. And I have to agree with you;

Autumn Leaves *is* a dump. And between you and me, I can barely tolerate Mr. Reemes—or Mr. Prescott. Oh, he's the owner."

"I know," she said, grinning. "I've met him."

He snickered again and raised an eyebrow. "You do seem to get around. Anyway, there's been a strong inside rumor for the past year that Mr. Reemes will be leaving, and if he goes, so will Mr. Prescott. I'm just biding my time here." He drank some tea. "Regardless, I want to be his replacement. We're actually pretty much on the same level as far as job titles go, and even though I've tried and tried to get changes made around here, Mr. Prescott has the final say." He swallowed more of the tea. "And the two of them are like glue, going off on cruises, and acting like big shots. I don't think they care, or even have a clue about the people here."

"But what about inspectors? Aren't they supposed to come around from time to time and check things out?"

"I've been back and forth with the state for months about that," he said, finishing his tea. "And there's never been any action taken—nothing. I can't understand it."

"But don't they write your paychecks?"

"Oh, no. I get paid from the Prescott-Lisser Group. Lauren does, too. They're actually the ones who run Autumn Leaves and other establishments in the southeast."

Mattie was all ears. For the first time, Harold Bates had opened up and confided in her. She then felt comfortable enough to reveal the incident with Gwen and the note she'd found.

Bates couldn't hide his outrage. "A note? *Thanks for your help*? I can't believe it! This is not good." He drank some more tea. "Well, I suppose you can't really prove much by a note, but it does makes you wonder. Mattie, don't you have a lawyer friend who comes to see you?"

She shook her head. "Yes—and I've already given him the note."

"Well, without a signature, it probably wouldn't mean much of anything, but it's certainly troublesome to me." He shook his head in disgust. Then suddenly, he remembered the phone call from the TV station and brightened as he gave her the information. "They want you, the dog and its owner, and Fae Munn, if possible; they want all of you to be here for the filming."

"Awesome! When are they coming?"

"The fifteenth. Next Tuesday."

Mattie thought for a moment. "But what about the conference?"

"What conference?"

"The conference with the owners of private homes and inns over in Winston-Salem, you know, where they all share ideas and suggestions on how to improve places like Autumn Leaves."

"But that's no conference," he told her. "That's just a bunch of nut cases who are looking for an excuse to get off work and go party somewhere."

She looked astonished, gazing at him. "But Reemes asked me to be our representative." Then slowly, she sat back in her chair and let out an, "Ohhh, I get it. Tell me, did Mr. Reemes know about the TV station calling you this morning?"

"Oh, sure; I saw him in the hall and told him. Why?"

"That miserable creep. I'll bet he's trying to keep me away from the TV people."

Harold Bates had a good laugh. "I'll bet you're right!" He paused, rubbing his chin, then said, "But hey, if he thinks you're not going to be here...why spoil his fun?"

Mattie was grinning. "I'm starting to like you, Harold. You think the way I do."

Leaning forward in his chair, he spoke softly while glancing over his shoulder at the door to make sure no one could hear. "Okay, Mattie; here's what we're going to do..."

Later that afternoon, Mattie and Clare were taking a stroll. Approaching them, a familiar figure called out, "Hello, girls." It was Gwen.

The women answered her in unison. "We're so glad you're back," Mattie said. "How are you doing?"

Gwen looked down, as if she were embarrassed. "I'm okay. Just have to take one day at a time." She looked at Mattie. "You knew I was in rehab?"

Mattie and Clare exchanged looks of surprise. "No, we hadn't heard."

Appearing remorseful, Gwen said, "I'm doing good—for now. Just hope I can keep it up." Approaching her room, she opened her door and told them how glad she was to be back. Mattie's curiosity got the better of her and she quickly peeked over toward Gwen's bed, which appeared clean and bottle-free.

"Gwen, if you ever need a helping hand or support or anything, you know you've got friends," Mattie said.

Surprisingly, Gwen embraced both of them. "That means a lot to me. Thanks, girls."

Strolling away, Clare said, "Think we should've told her about your last rally?"

Mattie frowned. "Maybe not yet. Let's let her try to get back into a routine first, don't you think, Clare?"

Clare nodded. "As long as that routine doesn't include secret visits from our pal, Reemes."

Then Mattie told her the story of how Mr. Reemes had approached her about the "conference" and how she and Harold Bates had discussed it and also the TV crew coming to Autumn Leaves on the same day.

Clare gave a snort. "Television? *Here?*"

"I know! But you didn't hear it from me," Mattie cautioned. "I don't know if they're going to announce it or just let it happen. We need to round up people for another outdoors game that day. Could you help me?" Clare nodded. "Oh, and we need to see if Jean can have Scooter here," Mattie went on. "Can you talk to her? I've got her phone number. It wouldn't be right not to have the dog here."

"Sure," Clare agreed; "I'll give her a call. The show can't go on without the star. But what about you? Where will you be?" Mattie gave her a mischievous smile and Clare stood back, one hand propped on a hip. "Whatcha' got cookin', Matts?"

Mattie blinked innocently. "I don't know what you mean, Clare." Then with one arm propped around her friend's waist, she lowered her voice and chattered away, while they strolled along.

It was Monday, the 14th. Mattie had been outside for her walk, when Mr. Reemes caught up with her in the lobby. "Mrs. Morgan; uh, ready for tomorrow?" He was jangling some keys in his pocket and seemed nervous.

Barely able to keep a straight face, Mattie said, "Oh, yes; I'm all set for tomorrow." And she continued down the hall toward her room. Glancing over her shoulder, she saw him watching her, and she chuckled to herself.

Mattie had noticed some small improvements in the halls of Autumn Leaves in preparation for the television crew next day. All of the burned out light bulbs in the halls and in the lobby had been replaced; the tile floors were shiny and the carpet had been vacuumed; even the windows shone brightly. "You can actually see out of them!" she told Harold Bates later, when he stopped by her room.

"We need to keep things looking like this, or better, all the time," he said, as if in apology. Then he asked quietly, "You're good to go?"

"Oh, yes. I know the plan. I'll be waiting for your call, Harold."

He nudged her arm with his elbow and said almost gleefully, "I can't wait!"

Tuesday, the 15th, arrived. Mattie stayed in her room all morning, with the door closed. After lunch, Clare rounded up some of the others and gathered them outside for a Frisbee toss. While they were wrapped up in the game, Mattie watched the fun from her window. She hoped desperately that Mr. Reemes wouldn't show up in the yard and spoil everything.

Her phone rang. It was Harold Bates. After a couple of "uh-huhs" and "okays" she hung up and said excitedly, "Here we go!"

The T.V. crew came in toting a camera and dragging some wiring. Harold Bates greeted Kerrie Kane in the lobby and she introduced him to her cameraman. Jim Reemes stood unnoticed back by a side door where he could hear everything without being part of anything.

Jean had arrived with Scooter on a leash and Bates introduced her and the puppy to Ms. Kane, who gave a direction to the cameraman, and the interview began.

"We're talking with Jean McGraw who's the owner of this little guy," Kerrie Kane said, reaching down and petting Scooter. "How has your life been affected by Scooter coming into Autumn Leaves, Ms. McGraw?"

"Well, after I heard about Mattie and Clare bringing him in to a woman here who'd had a stroke," Jean said, "I knew we had to get him up to a place in Asheville where he's now in a training program for dogs to work with the handicapped."

"Wonderful! Could we talk with the women?"

Hearing that, Jim Reemes gave a self-righteous snicker. "Don't you wish," he muttered (no doubt with pride at his own cleverness at having gotten Mattie out of the way).

At that point, Ms. Kane noticed the game going on in the back yard. She asked Harold Bates if she could take the camera out to the area. He beamed proudly and extended his hand for her to follow ahead of him. Mr. Reemes scowled at hearing that, not yet aware of anything going on out back.

When they reached the porch, the reporter began again. Some of the residents noticed and waved to the camera. "This is wonderful, Mr. Bates," she said. "Do things like this happen often?"

"Occasionally. When Mrs. Morgan organizes them, that is."

"She's the woman who brought the dog in for the woman with the stroke?" He nodded. "But where is she? Can we meet her?"

Jim Reemes nearly laughed aloud, as he tagged along, unobtrusively behind the others; just to make sure things were going as he had planned—*without* Mrs. Morgan.

At the same time, Clare, who'd been in the yard leading most of the boisterous fun, started up a cheer. "Where's Mattie? We want Mattie! We want Mattie!"

"Someone call me?" It was a beaming Mattie, who had sneaked outside and was standing on the porch where everyone, including Mr. Reemes, could see her clearly.

His jaw dropped a mile and his eyes glazed over like an icy windshield. Mattie came right over to him and without missing a beat, introduced him to Kerrie Kane and the WYMT television audience.

Ms. Kane turned to him and spoke into a microphone, "You must be so proud of Mrs. Morgan!"

Mr. Reemes' cough caught up with him again, and he sputtered a few words, while Ms. Kane looked on, perplexed, to say the least.

Clare showed up then with a big smile plastered on her face. "Here's the puppy, Mattie," she called out.

Mattie kept the ball rolling for the camera. "Why, there's Scooter, the little dickens." And she reached down, picked up the tail-wagging puppy, and handed him over to Mr. Reemes, who looked startled, as if he'd just been handed a live grenade. "Don't you just love dogs?" she asked him brightly. "Especially dogs that help our folks here. Isn't that right, Mr. Reemes?"

He drew back, looking most uncomfortable, and somehow managed a feeble, trembling smile, then returned the dog to Mattie, all for the enjoyment of the viewing audience.

Ms. Kane, confused by his reaction, kept up the interview. "Could you take us to the woman who had the stroke?" She gave a signal to the cameraman to cut, while she and the others strolled together with Jean and the dog down the hall towards Fae Munn's room. Mr. Reemes excused himself nervously with some lame excuse about having some work to do.

Approaching Fae's room, Mattie got a real surprise. Fae wasn't in her bed! "Where's Fae?" she called out. "Did she go back to the hospital?!"

"She's right here." It was Lauren. She'd been standing on the other side of the room, with Fae, who was sitting up in a chair! And smiling a little crookedly, but smiling nevertheless.

"Fae!" Mattie cried out, sucking in a big breath. "Look at you!"

"You're out of bed!" Clare chimed in. With her hands on her hips, she said, "You'll be running around the block before long!"

Fae's only response was a big grin. Mattie turned to Lauren and introduced her to the TV people. "But how'd Fae do this?" Mattie wanted to know.

Lauren was beaming and spoke aside quietly to Mattie. "We had to let the other aide go. Mr. Bates thought she wasn't working out, so he asked if I'd step in and help Mrs. Munn in my spare time."

"So that's where you've been keeping yourself lately. And you didn't say a word!"

Lauren smiled slyly as Mattie hugged her and said, "Well, this certainly is a wonderful surprise."

Ms. Kane stayed in the background for a moment, giving the women privacy while they spoke. Finally, she asked if they could let Fae hold the puppy for the cameras. Scooter behaved like a lovable little guy while Fae petted him. Even Mattie could sense a difference in the dog as soon as he got up on Fae's lap. She stepped aside, allowing Fae and Scooter to be the center of attention, which she felt they so well deserved.

After the crew, Jean, and Scooter had left, Harold Bates stayed in the lobby with Mattie and Clare. "We pulled it off, didn't we?!" he said, exchanging high fives with them.

"Did you see the look on Mr. Reemes' face when Mattie handed him the dog?" Clare spouted. "I nearly wet my...I mean, I nearly lost it!"

"I'll probably be in trouble, again," Mattie said, rolling her eyes.

Jim Reemes had been waiting in his office with the door partly ajar and overheard. "You bet you'll be in trouble," he muttered.

Mary A. Berger

 **14**

The next day, Mattie went looking for Mr. Bates to go over the events with the TV crew. When she arrived at his office, she saw a note posted on his door: "Gone to Charlotte—Back Tomorrow."

She sagged a little, but started outside for her walk. The sky had turned from soft blue to grey, with dark clouds building. She noticed it was just starting to rain. Within moments, the sprinkles had turned to a serious gully-washer, complete with high winds and torrents of rain.

"Better not head out in this," she muttered, wandering back across the lobby. Mattie loved—no—needed her walks. They restored her and left her feeling newly energized. So when she missed a walk, she often felt a little bored.

She spent the rest of the day visiting with some of the residents, many of whom were from the other side of the center. And, of course, much of the conversation centered on the goings-on of the day before. Most everyone she talked to seemed happier, brighter, she noticed. Good things were starting to happen; Mattie could sense it.

As she approached her room, the phone was ringing and she rushed to answer it. It was Clare. "Clare? How come you're calling me on the phone?"

"I'm at the airport," she said. "My daughter's in the hospital. I tried all afternoon to get hold of you. I had to leave in such a hurry because there's only one flight to Columbus going out today."

"Oh, Clare; I'm so sorry. But how's your daughter? I hope it's nothing serious."

"They think she might have had a mild heart attack. They're keeping her in the hospital for a few days, running tests, doing all kinds of procedures and things. But the good news is she may be coming home by the weekend."

"You must be relieved about that."

"Oh, yes. But Mattie, do you know how I heard about it? My grandkids—you know; the scary teenagers? They called me and asked if I would come. I couldn't believe it! They have family and friends all around but they actually wanted me." She sounded as if she were close to tears.

"See, Clare, when the chips are down, who do they call? Good old Grandma! But listen; is there anything I can do while you're gone?" Mattie asked.

"Just let Mr. Bates and some of the others know, okay?"

"Will do. I'm so glad you called. Keep me posted, Clare. And I do hope everything goes well with your daughter."

They hung up and Mattie went to make tea. It felt a little odd knowing Clare wasn't around, but she knew Clare was headed to where she had to be.

Once the storm passed, Mattie managed to get her walk in. Back in her room, she went right to her computer and sent off an email to Jed. She remembered he had a big case today, so she knew he wouldn't be back in touch until late tomorrow, at the earliest. Then she picked up a newspaper and glanced at the sports section to see how her Braves were doing.

She heard a tap at her door. When she looked up, a medic was standing in the doorway. Mattie recalled him as the overbearing aide who'd suffered the blow from her cane on her first day there. "Mrs. Morgan?" He looked as if he was still miffed at her—even after several months.

She let the newspaper slide into her lap. "Yes? What is it you want?"

"I have a message from Mr. Reemes." The guy's expression appeared almost arrogant. "He'd like to see you in his office."

I knew this was coming, Mattie thought. She then informed the messenger, "Look, you tell Mr. Reemes if he wants to see me, he knows where I live."

The medic gave a disgusted "tsk," turned around, and left in a huff.

In Reemes' office, Jim Reemes couldn't help spouting off at Wynn Prestcott about what happened with the TV crew the day before and how Mattie' had shown up regardless of his attempt to keep her away. "That woman has gone too far, way too far!"

Prestcott snuffed out a cigarette in an ashtray on Mr. Reemes' desk. "Too bad she's so easy on the eyes. Makes it harder to, you know, keep her in line."

Reemes calmed down a little. "She is a looker. Nice body, nice eyes. That's about the only reason she's lasted this long here: I like watching her walk. But right now I'm so damned furious with her acting as if she's running the place. Well, I won't have that!" he stormed, pounding his desk.

"Besides, we've got everything going our way here," Prestcott said. "Nobody climbing down our backs. Vacations whenever we want, golf outings, time off; and it all comes out of these idiots' pocketbooks." He shot Reemes a piercing look. "Oh yeah, Jim, you've gotta do something about that woman, and soon."

"But we have to be careful, Wynn. I hear she has a lawyer friend and—"

Prestcott sagged. "Oh, great. That's all we need. Some nosy-ass lawyer hanging around. Well, we'll just give her a little scare. Just enough to get the message across. Agreed?"

Reemes nodded. Just then, the medic returned with Mattie's blunt message. Both Reemes and Prestcott headed for Mattie's, vengeance in their eyes.

At Mattie's room, they didn't bother knocking. "Mrs. Morgan!" Jim Reemes snapped, as the two men paraded across the room right over to where she was sitting. "Exactly what is going on?"

Mattie blinked innocently. "What are you talking about?"

The men towered over her, standing on either side. Mr. Prestcott spoke. "Mrs. Morgan, I believe we've met. And I believe you know exactly what Mr. Reemes is talking about." Crossing his arms, his eyes glaring, he went on. "Seems you like to run things here at Autumn Leaves. We don't really appreciate that. Mr. Reemes and I run things here."

"And Mr. Bates," Mattie added. "Don't forget him."

"Yes, and Mr. Bates isn't here to help you this time, now is he?" Jim Reemes said, reminding her of their earlier confrontation, when Harold Bates had stepped into his office in the middle of things.

"Aw, c'mon, guys," said Mattie, "lighten up. Everything turned out just great with the television people, and Autumn Leaves looks like a slice of heaven," she added, rolling her eyes.

"What are you both so upset about?"

Jim Reemes reached into his shirt pocket and pulled out a piece of paper, unfolded it and shoved it under nose. It was one of Mattie's flyers. "Look familiar?" he asked, leering.

She swallowed hard but managed to stay calm. "Of course it does." She gave a deep sigh. "Look, I've told you before and I'll tell you again. These people need more than they're getting here. I just wanted to help them. They're human beings, for crying out loud!"

With that, she started to get up from her chair. But Reemes and Prescott blocked her way. Mattie sat back, a startled look in her eyes.

"We will take care of the people's needs here," Wynn Prescott said.

"Oh, that's really working, now isn't it?" she came back.

"That will be enough out of you!" Prescott yelled. "Look, we don't want any more trouble, Mrs. Morgan! Do you understand?" Mattie sat silently. "Do you?!" he thundered.

Mattie tried to reach for her phone. Again, she was blocked by the men.

"What are you trying to do?!" she cried out. "I'm not your prisoner!" At that, she managed to slip out of the chair and head for her door. Two hands slammed the door shut before she could reach it. Slowly, she backed away from them, growing fear reflecting in her eyes.

"I think you get the message, don't you, Mrs. Morgan?" Prescott asked, still glaring.

"I'll bet she does, Wynn," Jim Reemes said.

Mattie didn't know what to expect next. But she knew was she had to do something. All of a sudden, she began screaming at the top of her voice, pounding the walls with her fists and running around her room like a crazed flamenco dancer, even snatching up her whistle and blowing it wildly.

The men's eyes popped open in surprise. "What the hell?" Wynn Prescott wailed.

"She's gone nuts!" Reemes yelled, and both men turned tail and ran from the room.

Gasping in anger and fear, Mattie slammed her door shut, locked it, and then leaned back against it until she could catch her breath. In spite of having driven them off, she was shaking. Don't panic, she told herself. Just don't panic. She inhaled a few deep breaths and gradually felt calm enough to use the phone. Instinctively, she dialed Jed's number. Four rings. No answer. Then his voice mail kicked in.

"J, Jed. It's Mattie. Would you call me when you get a chance?" She fought to control her voice. Regardless, Jed probably wouldn't get to her message until tomorrow. She thought of phoning Scotty, and then remembered he was taking Lauren to dinner and a ball game. She went to see Clare but forgot she was away.

Slumping, close to tears, Mattie returned to her room, locking the door behind her. She hadn't even eaten any supper; and right now she didn't feel like supper. Instead, she changed into her pajamas, crawled into bed and pulled the covers up over her head. She kept seeing the images of Reemes and Prescott (large men that they were) hovering over her, truly frightening her.

"What kind of jailhouse is this?!" she spouted aloud. "Who do they think they are?! Oh, Lord, what am I gonna' do?!" she cried out in a prayer of desperation. It was too much for Mattie. For the first time at Autumn Leaves, she buried her face in her pillow, and cried herself to sleep.

Later, the phone ringing startled her and sent her into a panic. She looked at the clock. Two-thirty in the morning.

Heart pounding, she reached for the phone and managed a shaky, "Hello?"

It was Jed. "Mattie, are you all right?! I got your message. What's wrong?"

She swallowed hard. Finally, she said, "Jed, I know how busy you are right now. I shouldn't have called"

"You call me any time—night or day," he said emphatically. "My case ended earlier than

I expected. It's all over. I just got back from wrapping things up. Now tell me, please, what's wrong?"

Mattie felt a little better, hearing that his case was finished. She mentioned about the TV people coming, but when she went into the story about Reemes and Prescott and how they'd behaved earlier in her room, she nearly broke down.

"Did they lay a hand on you?!" Jed thundered.

"No . . . and I would've fought them off hard if they'd tried to. It's just that they wouldn't let me use my phone, or even allow me to leave my room!" Her voice began to crack, even though she fought for control.

Jed knew Mattie well enough to know it took a lot to get her this upset. But he also was smart enough to know he had to help her calm down. "Mattie," he said, lowering his voice, "everything will be all right. I have a friend who might be able to help us out here. Now I want to hear about these television people. They actually came out to the center?"

"Yes! Jed, it was wonderful." And she began filling him in on the details of the event. By the time they'd talked a while longer, she sounded and felt better. She could sense the concern and comfort in his voice, so soothing and reassuring. Then he promised he'd be down as soon as he could get there.

"This distance between us is getting to me," he told her half-jokingly, then added quickly, "but I'm not about to let it stop me."

"Oh, Jed; hearing your voice is just what I needed right now. I'm so glad you called."

"Even if it is the middle of the night?"

She laughed and said, "I don't care! I'm just glad you called."

"I am, too. I'll see you soon. Good night, dear Mattie."

"Good night," she said, smiling.

 15

Jed paced the floor in his study, thankful he got Mattie calmed down. He brewed a pot of coffee and drank almost the whole pot. Stretching out on his bed, he fell in and out of sleep.

By nine o'clock next morning, he was on the phone. "Rocco? How's it going, pal? This is Jed Mitchell."

"Mr. Mitchell! Good to talk to ya'. What's happenin' man?"

"Oh, I need a little favor, Rocco."

"Heyyy, after all you done for me, I owe ya—big time. I mean, you got me outta' the slammer, for cryin' out loud!"

"Well, you shouldn't have been there in the first place. Let's just say I know a set-up when I see one. We had to take care of that."

"Hey, man, I'll owe ya for the rest of my life. My ol' lady sez the same t'ing. Whatcha' want from me? You name it; you got it."

They talked for a while longer, and then Jed thanked him and said, "I'll be in touch."

Then he went to his organizer and flipped through some phone numbers. "Here it is. Autumn Leaves. Jim Reemes. Now where's that number for Prescott? Ah, here it is..."

Two days later, Jim Reemes sat nervously in his office, while Wynn Prescott paced the floor in front of Reemes' desk. "What do you suppose they want?" asked Reemes, his face pale as he tapped his fingers nervously on the desk.

"I don't know, but any time you hear from Raleigh, it can't be good." Prescott smashed out a cigarette. "I don't like any of this. And we can't be taking chances, Jim. You know how that would look."

"What's taking them so long? They were supposed to be here twenty minutes ago."

"Calm down. The last thing we need is to look worried. I'm sure they won't suspect. "

A tap at the door interrupted their conversation. "Good morning, gentlemen. My name is Jed Mitchell. I'm an attorney and I'm here to speak with both of you."

Jim Reemes and Wynn Prescott exchanged questioning looks, and then Prescott said, "An attorney? Are you with the state?"

Jed smiled confidently and shook his head. "No, no. I'm not with the state."

"But we thought—"

"I know," Jed said. "I wanted you both here. Sorry if I derailed your golf plans or any other plans you had for today." Without asking, he took a seat at Reemes' desk.

"What *is* this?" demanded Prescott, his hands propped defiantly on his waist. "Why are you here?"

Jed held up a finger. "One second," he said and turned toward the door, which he had purposely left partway open. "Rocco? Rocco, are you there?"

A giant of a man, big as a tank, stepped up to the door. His long, black hair was pulled back into a ponytail, and surrounding a wild beard were several body piercings on his mouth, nose, and up his ears. His massive tree-trunk arms bore wild tattoos. A ragged, sleeveless t-shirt hung loosely over torn blue jeans, while dark, piercing eyes emitted an evil glare that would've made a terrorist shudder.

"I don't like doors," the man named Rocco growled, looking straight ahead at the office door. "Reminds me of bein' in the slammer!"

Suddenly, and with Herculean strength, he grabbed hold of the door, let out a blood-curdling roar, and in one fast movement ripped the door right off its hinges and slammed it to the floor, making a thunderous racket.

Drawing back in shock, Mr. Reemes and Mr. Prescott stood paralyzed by what had just happened.

"Oh, dear," Jed said, sitting back and shaking his head. "Rocco, I told you that you shouldn't do things like that." He turned to the men, who were still gawking. "Don't worry," Jed assured them, "we'll take care of the damages." Then he looked them straight in the eyes. "Mr. Reemes, Mr. Prescott, there's something Rocco and I would like to get straight."

In spite of their own height, Rocco stood, towering over the men, his breathing heavy, like dragon's breath, while he flexed his mammoth arms and glared. Jed went on. "I believe you two paid a visit to a Mrs. Morgan the other day?" Standing with their mouths wide open,

Reemes and Prescott remained in shocked silence, while Jed went on. "She tells me you were a little threatening to her. Is this true?"

In that moment, the two men lost every ounce of arrogance. "Oh, no, no; there, there must be some mistake," Reemes stammered.

"That's not the way I heard it," Jed said, shaking his head. "Rocco, let's all go pay Mrs. Morgan a visit. What d'you say?"

Glaring down at the men, Rocco hissed, "Youse guys comin' or do I hafta'?" Both men scrambled to attention, nearly tripping over each other. Wynn Prescott, his face white with fear, walked quickly and gingerly around the big guy, while Jim Reemes sort of slithered his way along the wall, stepping over the flattened door, not daring to take his eyes off the animal-man named Rocco.

With Rocco's giant hands on each of their shoulders, the silent Mr. Reemes and Mr. Prescott walked like truant eighth-graders on their way to the principal's office. Approaching Mattie's room, Jed turned to Rocco and said quietly, "I think you've done your job. You can go now." Rocco nodded, not taking his eyes off Reemes and Prescott.

"Thanks, Buddy," Jed said, patting Rocco's shoulder, and knowing some day he would have to tell Mattie about him.

"Hey-y-y, no problem, Mr. Mitchell. Just let me know if youse need me for anyt'ing else." Rocco then gave Reemes and Prescott a final, sickening sneer.

Jed tapped on Mattie's door. "Mrs. Morgan, may we come in?"

Watering her plants, Mattie's mouth dropped open at seeing Jed, Mr. Reemes, and Mr. Prescott together. "Jed, what a...nice surprise..." she muttered, frowning with uncertainty.

"I believe these men owe you an apology, Mrs. Morgan," Jed said, in charge and sounding much the lawyer. Turning to the men, he folded his arms across his chest, glared at them and said deliberately through clenched teeth, "The lady is waiting."

Mr. Prescott took the lead and began apologizing profusely, his words coming out almost in garbled form, and Mr. Reemes joined in right behind him.

"What we did was very wrong, very wrong, indeed, Mrs. Morgan," he said, his voice trembling. He glanced over a shoulder out to the hall, as if checking to see if the gorilla, Rocco, were still hanging around.

Still somewhat confused, Mattie muttered, "It's . . . all right." But in an instant the memory flashed through her mind of a few nights earlier when it hadn't been "all right." Stepping closer to the men, her expression changed, and her eyes turned to ice. "Wait a minute," she said, squinting. "No, no; it is not alright. You came into my room, my own room, and treated me like some sort of *prisoner*. How dare you! How dare you!" And she began beating on both their chests with her fists and crying fiercely, "How dare you!!"

Taking her punches, the men looked helplessly at Jed. Jed simply shrugged and gave them an innocent gee-fellas-what-do-you-want-me-to-do look.

After taking Mattie's wrath, the men actually sounded genuinely repentant. "I am sorry, Mrs. Morgan. I know you're just trying to help your friends here." It was Mr. Prescott.

"Me, too," added Jim Reemes. "Don't worry, Mrs. Morgan. It won't happen again."

"You're damned right it won't!" Jed bellowed at the men. Arms still crossed, he turned his back to them and with a nod to the door said, "You two can leave now." And both Reemes and Prescott slithered out of the room, dragging their cowardly tails behind.

Mattie stood momentarily gazing at Jed. "Wow," she finally murmured, as they went to each other's arms in their usual way, embracing affectionately. Her eyes were huge, staring up at him in admiration.

"Jed . . . you were wonderful. How can I ever thank you?"

"I can think of one way," he said tenderly, drawing her close. She felt his lips on hers and gave a tiny gasp. Then, looking up into his eyes and melting, Mattie kissed him back.

 16

A few days later, Jed walked into the Asheville police station. The old halls echoed when he spoke to the officer in charge, who sat behind an old oak desk.

"How's it going, buddy?"

"Okay. Say, have you heard anything more about that Eva woman?"

"Nope, haven't heard a word from her," Jed told him truthfully. His expression turned to one of anger. "But I'd like to hear what Mr. Owen Black has to say. When's he due?"

"Some time this afternoon," the officer answered. But I don't think you'll be able to see him."

"What? Why not? My assistant called and said I was needed here."

"I know, Jed. I told her to call you, myself. But when the chief got word of all this, he wanted to bring Owen Black in on his own. He won't let you within ten feet of him."

"We'll see about that," Jed said, his face showing determination.

It was almost a half hour later, when chief Bill Weaver showed up with none other than the louse, Owen Black. Black had lost some weight and looked disheveled, with his thinning hair hanging down in strings around his face. He was wearing some grimy blue jeans and scuffed sandals.

Chief Weaver took him into a private office and Jed was quick to follow. "Hey Billy Boy, who've you got there? Why, if it isn't that man himself, Mr. Owen Black," Jed said, his voice unfriendly, to say the least. Jed motioned for the chief to step out into the hall. They chatted quietly for a few moments, and then Jed followed him back into the room. Before entering, Jed gave a "thumbs up" to the officer at the front desk, who sat shaking his head in disbelief.

Bill Weaver sat opposite Black at a small table and motioned for Jed to take a seat as well. "What in hell's the matter with you, Black?!" he roared. "How could you get yourself into such a mess?"

Owen Black said nothing.

"You got taken in, didn't you, Mr. Black?" Jed asked. "By the calendar girl, Eva. Isn't that right? She threw herself at you and for some unknown reason, you couldn't resist her, uh, 'charms'. Didn't you stop to think about your future; jail, probably—losing your license, for certain. Come on, Owen," Jed coaxed, "talk to me."

"I'm not talking to anybody," Owen growled.

"Oh, sure you are," Chief Weaver said. He got up, walked over to Black's side of the table, and sat on the edge, facing him. "What you've done is illegal, and you know it. Using that old will when you knew there was a new one; I mean, come on! Not only did your girlfriend lose you on the island, buddy, she set you up so you'd get arrested and she's free as a bird!" He leaned forward and got right in Owen's face. "Damn it! You tell us what happened or—"

"Or *what?*" Owen said with a smirk. "I'm not telling you anything!"

Jed could see they were getting nowhere with that approach. "Er, Owen, would it make a difference if I told you we got our hands on Eva?" he said, stretching the truth. "And she sang like a diva when we told her she'd go to jail same as you."

"You're lying. You don't even know where she is!"

Jed smiled confidently. "Oh, yeah. Well, we do. In fact, she told us all about Mrs. Morgan's car, and about how she *disposed* of it. She also mentioned some things that were in the Morgan's safe at their house, and how you talked her into getting rid of —"

"She told you that? That bitch! Wait'll I get my hands on her! She promised me she'd keep it quiet."

With a cunning smile, Jed looked over at Chief Weaver. "There you go, Chief. That should be good for a start."

Suddenly, Black clammed up. Unfortunately for the chief and Jed, just as Owen sounded as if he were about to reveal more, he caught himself. "I'll be my own lawyer," he told them arrogantly. With that, the still fuming Owen Black slunk back in his chair.

Chief Weaver motioned for Jed to follow him out to the hall. Closing the door, Jed turned to the chief. "Damn!" he said, frowning; "a few more minutes and we might even have gotten a confession out of him, the way he took the bait on us finding Eva."

"Oh, you really didn't find her?"

"Not yet," Jed admitted. "But Owen Black didn't know that, did he?"

"Good strategy, Jed," Chief Weaver said. Looking defeated, then, he added, "but this guy's not about to let himself be dragged into anything." He looked over at Jed. "I hope you know what you're doing. You're a good man,

Jed; one of the best in fact." He shook his head. "It's just that we were so close."

"Like they say, close only counts in horseshoes."

Later that afternoon, Jed called Mattie. "Mattie. It's so good to hear your voice. I'd like to drive down there and take you to dinner tonight. How about it?"

Mattie was excited. "Of course, Jed. That sounds wonderful!"

"Great. I'll pick you up around six. See you then."

Wearing white sandals and a white sundress with splashes of colorful flowers, she greeted him at the door.

"Look at you, pretty lady!" he complimented her. They greeted each other with their usual embrace and he kissed her softly.

Gathering her purse, Mattie spouted, "Well, come on; tell me about Owen Black!"

"Let's talk about it over dinner, okay? There's a wonderful old inn I'd like to take you to, overlooking a mountain golf course; if that's all right with you?

"Heavenly!" And they left and headed out in Jed's rental car.

At the front of the inn, four stucco pillars at the double doors greeted visitors beyond a wrought iron gate. Huge window boxes overflowed with summer pansies and other plantings beneath large picture windows, which overlooked a pristine golf course. When Jed pulled into the brick-lined drive, a valet stepped out to park his car.

Jed and Mattie went inside the front lobby, with its fine oak paneling and slate floor. Beyond that, they could see a softly lit dining room with plush carpet and lead glass chandeliers that hung from an old, stamped tin ceiling.

Once inside the dining room, a pleasant hostess seated them in a booth overlooking the golf course, framed by a broad, rolling view of the Blue Ridge mountains in the background.

"Mmm, nice," Mattie said, enjoying the view. "You can see forever!"

"Mattie, would you like a glass of wine?"

"Oh, yes; white would be nice."

Jed ordered a glass of Pinot Grigio for each of them and when it was delivered, told the server not to be in a hurry taking their order. They raised their glasses and Jed gazed at her but said simply, "To us, Mattie."

"To us," she repeated, "clinking" her glass against his. Not one to waste any time, she blurted out, "Okay, now let's hear about Owen Black."

"Mattie," Jed said. "The guy's a first-class rat. He's giving all of us a hard time. He finally just clammed up and said he didn't have to tell us a thing." He shook his head. "I wish I could tell you more about it, but there's not much to tell, even now. We have him in custody, but he refuses to talk."

Mattie sagged. "So we still don't know what happened with Gabe's papers, the contents of the safe, or our wills?"

Jed looked somber as he reached over and took her hand. "We don't think he ever probated the will after Gabe died."

"What?! How can that be, Jed?"

"We think Owen and your stepdaughter flew the coop using Gabe's old will that left everything to her, of course. Then, as administrator, Eva got all she could get her hands on, without Black even bothering with your new wills. It could be considered criminal conspiracy."

Mattie had one hand on her forehead, trying to comprehend everything Jed was saying. "But that's illegal! He'll lose his license!"

"That would be a good thing. What we need to do is to get Eva here, madder than a wet cat, and put the two of them up against each other to get to the bottom of this."

"So everything really does belong to Eva?"

"Temporarily. That's why he took off with her; she had the money. And she needed him in order to get the money." He took another swallow of the wine. "But Mattie, please bear with me a little longer. It's not over; I guarantee you that. You know, I once told you we had people working on finding Eva. We still do." He toyed with the wine glass. "No, it's definitely not over." He was looking adoringly at her. "I hate to see you going through all this. I hate it."

Mattie could see the anguish in his eyes. "Jed, if you say it's not over, I believe you. We'll just have to hang on and hope your 'people' find Eva." She took a swallow of her wine, then reached over and patted his hand.

He was looking straight at her. "Mattie, you are amazing. What would I do without you?"

"I don't know what I'd do without *you*, Jed."

He took her hand in his. "Remember what I told you at your place? That hasn't changed. I'm still so crazy about you." Jed's eyes were locked on hers. She smiled as he went on. "But I don't want you to feel, well, obligated to me because I'm handling your case. I wouldn't want that."

Her eyes grew large. "Oh, no, Jed. I don't feel that way at all. Of course, I appreciate everything you've done for me." She let out a sigh of frustration. "I'd probably be a basket case if I didn't know you were working on things.

But you and I are best friends, aren't we?" He nodded and Mattie said, "Well, best friends help each other, don't they?"

"I know, Mattie, I know." He shrugged. "I'm not sure what I'm trying to say. I just don't want you to feel that you, well, that you 'owe' me." His eyes got that intense look again.

"Jed," she said weakly, her voice a half octave higher. She cleared her throat and began again. "Jed, the way I feel when you look at me has nothing to do with 'owing' you." She swallowed hard as they locked onto each other's eyes, his face glowing at what she said.

Just then, the server stopped by. "Are we ready to order?" Without taking her eyes off Jed, Mattie replied, "Ohh, yeahhh."

Squaring themselves, and hastily glancing at the menus while the server smiled to herself, they each ordered the rib-eye special with mashed potatoes and salad.

Mattie then began telling him about some of her experiences at the center; about how she'd finagled the paper and markers; how she'd met up with Hank the groundskeeper; the miserable weed lecture; and how she'd chased the speaker away.

Jed laughed heartily. "I can see you doing that," he told her, his smile full with fondness.

"It's good to see you laughing," she told him. "In the past, you've sometimes seemed a little...*distant*, I guess you'd say.

"Lonely is more like it, Mattie, especially after Ruth passed away." He had a somewhat troubled expression, and added, "Even though she was always working on her sewing, at least she was company."

"Ruth always struck me as the loner type," Mattie said, sipping more of her wine. "I guess I just didn't take time to get to know her."

Jed shrugged. "I sometimes felt as though I didn't know her, myself. She never seemed happy, Mattie. So I thought it must have been something I was doing or not doing that made her feel that way. Even though I tried to get her to talk about it, or open up, I blamed myself for not being a better husband." He looked down into his wine glass. "Maybe that's why I never married again." He looked at Mattie, who was taking in every word. "After Ruth, I simply thought I wasn't good marriage material."

Mattie wasn't going to let him think that. "Jed, I can't imagine that! You can't blame yourself. Ruth was just a different person, that's all. Some people are exuberant and happy, while others are...*quiet*." Mattie was trying to sound tactful. "She liked her sewing." And Mattie thought to herself how unfair it was of Ruth to treat him so shabbily.

"She liked her sewing more than she liked me, I can assure you," said Jed.

"Now how can you say that?"

He lowered his voice. "Well, Ruth didn't like me to...touch her, if you know what I mean."

Mattie nearly choked on her drink. Was the woman out of her mind?!" she wanted to squeal, but said calmly instead, "I had no idea, Jed. Do you suppose her illness finally destroyed her reasoning? Or her feelings?"

"That's possible. I hadn't thought of it that way. I always assumed it was my fault."

"Well, if you ask me," Mattie said, once again her outspokenness taking over, "I think any woman would be crazy to not want to be with you or " She inhaled a small breath, realizing what she'd just said. Their eyes met, and for a brief moment Jed and Mattie exchanged a meaningful, yet unspoken message.

All during dinner, they continued chatting and laughing and carrying on like the good friends they were. Then, to round things off, they ordered coffee.

"That was superb!" Mattie chirped after they'd finished. "But the best part was being here with you, Jed, just being together," she said, smiling and sipping the last of her coffee.

"I'll say! Uh, Mattie, how would you like to take a drive?" Jed asked, while tending to the dinner check. "There's a spot not too far from here, where we could catch the sunset."

To their surprise, when they got outside it was already dark.

"Jed, why don't we just go back to my place?" Mattie said. Of course, he agreed.

They got into his car, making a promise to return to the inn again soon. "Mattie, I'm so tired of all this coming and going with the case. I can't wait until it's over and I can spend more time with you."

Her heart racing at hearing that, she told him, "You will, Jed, and soon, I know it." They sat in the car and talked for a while longer. Jed was smoothing the steering wheel as he spoke. "You know, I've been giving things a lot of thought lately. I'm thinking of bowing out of my full-time practice, and just working as a consultant, more or less; and turning over most of my cases to my partner."

"Really, Jed?" Mattie could barely hold back her curiosity.

"Yes, really. I'd like to be able to do some of the things I want, instead of being tied down with one client after another. Does that make any sense to you?"

"Absolutely. I think everyone reaches that point in their career. I know Gabe did."

She gave a little shrug. "That's why we ended up down here. But you probably already knew that." He nodded and she went on. "You have to do what you have to do, Jed," she told him, happy that he was including her in his decision making.

He took her hand in his and kissed it, then gave her that look, and Mattie fought the urge to fan herself. Before pulling out of the drive, he looked over at her and gave her one last smile as they drove off.

Back inside her room, Jed took her in his arms and kissed her warmly. "Mattie," he said tenderly, "there's something I want to ask you."

"What, Jed?"

"I, I don't know exactly how to ask you. Mattie, when this is all over—"

Just then his cell rang. He cursed the phone, as did Mattie to herself, but just as he was about to turn it off, he saw it was from his assistant, Kathy. "I'm so sorry, Mattie. I'd better take this. She never calls unless it's very important."

Mattie just smiled and nodded.

"You *did?*" Jed cried out. "When? That's wonderful! Nice going! I'll get up there as soon as I can. Thank you, thank you!" He hung up and turned to Mattie, his eyes dancing.

"Sounds like good news," she said. "One of your cases?"

"Our case, Mattie. We got Eva!"

Mattie inhaled a deep breath. "I knew you'd do it! I just knew it! Thank the good Lord!"

Jed's eyes glowed with relief and without hesitation, he drew her into his arms again, and they kissed each other deeply.

"Oh, that was so nice," he said as they kissed once more. Then he let out a sigh of frustration. "I just get here and I have to leave you, again. But you heard me tell Kathy I'd be up in Asheville as soon as possible. That's where they're bringing Eva, back to the 'scene of the crime.' And I have a couple of things I absolutely must take care of right away to be prepared."

"So," said Mattie, "I guess you'll be leaving, *again*." They both said the word in unison. "Well, you'd better get going," she added. "Let's get this show on the road!"

They held each other tightly, and kissed good-bye. "I'll be back," he said tenderly. "Count on it."

As Jed walked down the hall, he noticed a light on in Jim Reemes' office and peered inside. Both Reemes and Prescott were there and Jed saw that the door had been re-hung from Rocco's "visit."

"'Evening, gentlemen," he greeted them. "Just making sure the door was taken care of." And he started to turn away.

But Jim Reemes had other plans. He sneered, "Yeah, well you better watch it, buddy; because we just might file a complaint against you for breaking and entering, the way you and your jailhouse pal came storming in here."

"Yes," Wynn Prescott added smugly, "we'll see you in court!"

Jed drew back, frowning. "Is that right?" He stepped into the office confidently. Then he drew out his billfold, reached into it, and showed them the note Mattie had found in Gwen's room. "Is this your handwriting, Mr. Reemes?"

Jim Reemes looked startled. "Where'd you get that?" he demanded.

"It was found in one of your residents' rooms, attached to a bottle of gin," Jed said pointedly. "The law states: Section Number 357, Article seven, Provision eleven, (he concocted) that establishments like Autumn Leaves must not put any resident in jeopardy, regarding alcohol or drug abuse, punishable by loss of license and possible jail sentencing." Then, he added a few more lawyerly terms to make it all sound convincing and serious.

Wynn Prescott glanced over at the note and gave a sarcastic sniff. "But it's not even signed!"

"Ah, but when we compare that writing to this..." Jed said, drawing out and unfolding a piece of paper he'd snatched on the sly from Reemes' desk when Rocco was there. "Is this your writing?" he asked Jim Reemes.

"Er, yes," Reemes answered, sounding a little shaky.

"I'm sure my handwriting expert will be able to investigate, and determine if the writing on the thank-you note matches yours," Jed said confidently. "And when he does, gentlemen, you'll see it doesn't matter that the note's not signed."

Both men's jaws dropped, and all Prescott could manage was a feeble, "Wh-what?"

"And if they match," Jed went on, "well, you know what that could mean." He cocked his head and added, "Now, what was it you were saying about wanting to take me to court?"

He returned the papers to his billfold and left with the two men staring dumbly, but not before hearing Wynn Prescott light into Jim Reemes, scolding him as though he were an unruly teenager.

Jed chuckled to himself. "Kids, today," he muttered.

 17

The next day, after Mattie had been out to "her" greenhouse, as Hank liked to call it, she returned to her room for a glass of cool water. She let out a "Whew!" as she flopped into her chair and blew a puff of air into that dangling curl that hung down. She was about to head for the shower, when she heard her name being called. It sounded like Clare!

"Is there anyone left in this graveyard?" It was Clare, all right.

"You're back!" Mattie squealed and hurried into her arms.

"Yeah," Clare said. "Got in late last night and slept most of the morning."

"I'm so glad to see you, Clare. I've really missed you!" Then Mattie stood back and eyed her friend. "Blue jeans! And a t-shirt! And look at your hair; it's so pretty!" Clare's fire-truck red hair had been colored a soft, natural, light brown. "What happened to you?!" Mattie spouted. "Did you go on Mega Bucks Make-over? You look fabulous!" They both laughed and Mattie said, "Well, tell me; how's your daughter doing?"

"Oh, Mattie," Clare said, taking over Mattie's lounge chair and casually propping her feet up on a small table, "she's back home and she feels great. They want her to get into an exercise program to get rid of a few extra pounds and also to help keep her in better shape. In fact," Clare went on, cozying back in the chair, "she even asked me to take my granddaughter, Kaitlynn, shopping."

"How fun!"

"Oh, yeah. But it ended up that Kaitlynn took me shopping. We had a ball! She told me

it was time to get out of those goofy muumuus I'd been wearing." With a chuckle, Clare said,

"Know what else she told me?" Mattie shook her head. "She's fifteen, mind you, and she said the way I was dressed, I looked like I should be out standing on a street corner!" They both laughed at that. "So she hunted for some clothes she thought would look good on me, things that were more . . . you know, more with it."

"Good for her," Mattie said.

"And we both had our hair done. I gave her some of my gold-red strands and she had them woven into her blonde hair!"

Mattie shook her head and chuckled. "That girl sounds like a free spirit."

"She sure is. And we had more LOLs together. That's 'laugh-out-loud' for those of you who are inexperienced with the texting world," she said in mock bragging.

"Well, ex-cuuuuuse me," Mattie came back. "But really, Clare, you look ten years younger." She went to refill her water glass and noticed that Clare wasn't carrying her usual "get through the day" drink and offered her some water.

"Oh, yes, thanks." And Clare let out a sigh. "You know, Mattie, for some strange reason it's actually good to be back. I've missed you a lot." She swallowed some water. "Now fill me in on what's been happening in this haven of happiness."

"Where to start . . .?" Mattie said. "But first of all, I'm so happy to hear about your daughter. That has to be a relief." Then she inhaled a deep breath and told Clare about the episode with Reemes and Prescott, how they'd come into her room and tried to bully her.

"Those bastards!" Clare snarled.

"Actually, Clare, I was really scared. And you know it takes a lot to frighten me. But do you know what I did when they wouldn't let me out of my room?"

"You turned into a police dog?"

"No!" Hattie said, frowning. "Are you ready for this? I started screaming and running around like a crazy person, and I even blew my whistle!"

"What?!"

"Well, it chased them away, didn't it?" And she added, "I'd always heard that if you feel threatened, do *something,*—make noise, anything. Well, I made some noise, all right!"

"Good girl, Matts! You are just too smart! No wonder I like hanging out with you. So what happened then?"

"Jed came in a day or so later with both of them, and made them apologize. He was amazing!" she said, rolling her eyes heavenward and smiling.

"Really?" Clare lowered an eyebrow and looked at her suspiciously. "Hmm. What's going on, Miss Mattie Patattie?" she asked, staring straight at her. "There's something in the air, I can tell. Now dish!"

"Oh, Clare. It's just that Jed's been so good to me and so helpful. I can hardly stop thinking about him!" She was gazing out the window.

"I wonder how he feels about you?"

Grinning, Mattie said, "Oh, he told me how he feels."

"And you?"

Mattie gave a sigh. "All I know is when he looks at me the way he does...I just want to melt."

"Well, it's no wonder," Clare came back, fanning herself with her hand. "He's so hot!" They were both giggling, and finally Clare grew serious. "Mattie...I think you're in love."

Mattie was still staring out the window. "Maybe I am." She turned back to Clare. "It feels so good." Her eyes began to well up as did Clare's, when they looked at each other.

Clare reached over and had her arms around her friend, both women tearful with joy. "Honey, I'm so happy for you!" They both reached for tissues and Clare said, "Girl, all I know is, I've never seen you like this before." Then she leaned forward, and with dancing eyes and a mischievous grin, said, "Tell me more!" And the two of them chatted for over an hour.

Their conversation was interrupted when Lillian stopped by Mattie's room. "Mattie, I'm so glad you're here!" She was visibly upset.

"What is it, Lillian? What's wrong?" Mattie asked, popping out of her chair.

"It's Gwen. They're taking her out. It doesn't look good. The emergency people are in her room now. I thought you'd want to know."

"Of course! I'll get right over there!" She and Clare scooted out of the room and headed for Gwen's, both silent.

When they arrived, they saw the 911 people guiding a covered stretcher, heading out through an emergency exit. One of the medics saw Mattie and shook his head.

"Good-bye, Gwen," Mattie whispered feebly, leaning against the wall. She noticed Harold Bates speaking with Lauren across the hall, while Mr. Reemes arrived on the scene.

"What happened to Gwen?" Mattie asked him.

"She passed away," Reemes said abruptly. "Now if you ladies will excuse me, I need to get some things out of her room."

Harold Bates came over behind Mr. Reemes and shook his head at Reemes' crude greeting to the women. "This is probably the most difficult time I have here," Harold told them,

"when someone leaves us. I'm so sorry. You knew Gwen had been sick, didn't you? Her body just couldn't handle it, poor thing." Looking at Mattie, he said, "It was all the drinking. Too much for one person." He and Mattie exchanged a knowing look of disgust, obviously regarding that note she'd told him about.

"She seemed to be doing so well," Mattie said. "She even came out to the greenhouse with us once and really enjoyed it."

"And she told us she was in rehab, too," Clare added. "I can't believe she's gone."

The women thanked Harold Bates for his concern and Mattie asked Clare to walk outside with her. But before they left, Mattie turned back to Harold and spoke with him for a few minutes. Clare saw him nodding his head and heard Mattie thanking him. Then the two women strolled outdoors, each in their own way expressing their sorrow over Gwen.

When they came back inside, Mattie nudged Clare. "Let's take a little stroll down this side hall. I've only been in this part once before, but there's something I need to check on."

Clare shrugged and said, "Okay, Detective Morgan."

As they reached the end of the hall, Mattie headed for what looked like a closet with its door ajar. Pushing the door open, she stepped inside, while Clare flipped on an overhead light.

Much larger than a closet, it appeared to be an old storage room with dust-covered benches, tables, lamps, a few folding chairs and ladders strewn about like a collection of stuff at a resale shop. A grimy bay window overlooked everything. Just then, Hank happened by.

"'Afternoon, ladies," he greeted them. "Need something?"

Mattie answered. "Oh, no, Hank. We're just being nosy. Tell me, is this room used for anything besides a junk yard?" Clare smiled to herself when she saw Mattie's wheels already spinning.

"Naw, it's not used at all. Nowadays, when we get old stuff, I just take it to the local charities or to them shops where they can sell it." Adjusting his cap, he said, "Some of this stuff's been here for years. Y'all wantin' to clean it up or somethin'?"

Mattie smiled shrewdly. "Maybe. If you might have time to give us a hand?"

Hank was more than willing. "Why, sure, Miss Mattie. You just let me know when, and I'll be here."

"Now?"

"Right now?" He looked surprised.

"I already spoke to Mr. Bates," she assured him, "and he said to go for it!"

With a shrug and both thumbs hooked behind the straps of his bib overalls, Hank said,

"Shoot, ain't got nothin' better to do. Sure, I'll help you."

"You in, Clare?" Mattie asked.

Clare gave a snicker. "Do I have any choice?" With a shrug, she said, "Oh well, I've always wanted to go trash pickin'." And she turned up the edges on the sleeves of her t-shirt. "Let's get to work!"

Between the three of them, they hoisted as much out of the room and into the hall as they could manage. Then Hank went and got his old garage vacuum. Though the carpet was old and damaged in places, it perked up with the vacuuming. While he did that, the women wiped off some of the benches and tables and lamps with old rags Hank had provided.

"Mattie?" Clare asked, suddenly curious, "what are we doing here? Getting ready for the next World's Fair?"

Mattie set her dust cloth down. "I'd like this to be a room for people like Gwen," she explained. "Sort of a sanctuary where anyone can come just to be alone, or to occasionally talk with someone who could try to help them with drinking problems, or other problems, or for people who just need to talk. Mr. Bates told me he knows a retired pastor who might be willing to volunteer his time."

Clare was silent for a moment. Then she looked Mattie in the eye and said sincerely, "Mattie, how do you do it? I mean, where do you get these ideas?"

Mattie simply shrugged. "You see a need, you try to help. That's all." Picking up her dust cloth, she said, "Now can you give me a hand with this table?"

They moved one of the little tables over to a corner, along with a lamp and a couple of chairs. Clare shook her head and watched in admiration, as her pal went buzzing around, fully engrossed in her new project.

"I'll be right back," Mattie told them, scooting off, then returning a few minutes later with a couple of plants from her room. "The place just needs some life," she said, smiling.

While the women wiped down the bay window, which had been covered with a haze of dust and grime, Hank found a couple of light bulbs and inserted them into the lamps. When he turned the lamps on, they set off a warm glow that seemed to penetrate the little room.

"We'll get these windows cleaned up better some other time," Mattie said, wincing at the streaks still there. "Maybe we can even find some curtains or blinds or something, and we'll get it painted, too."

The three of them stood back, rather impressed with what they'd just accomplished. Hank said he'd get rid of the ladders and the other things they didn't need.

"Miss Mattie," he said, "I couldn't help overhear what y'all told Miss Clare. Would you like a sign for this here room?"

"A sign?"

"Yep. I was thinkin' maybe something like Miss Gwen's Place. What d'y'all think?"

Mattie and Clare exchanged a look of delight, and Clare sucked in a big breath. "In honor of our fellow inmate!" And she raised her arms and gave a loud cheer.

"I think it's a wonderful idea, Hank!" Mattie told him.

Then both women embraced him, while he looked down and said, "Shucks, it was nothin'," but beaming all the while.

And so it was: the creation of Miss Gwen's Place.

As the three of them left, strolling along the hall, Mattie turned to Hank and said, "By the way, Hank, we'd like you to come in and put on a little program for us. You know, with your jokes and stories you like to tell. Would you be able to do that for us, maybe some day next week?"

Again, Hank looked down and beamed.

Clare resorted to begging. "Oh, please, Hank. We need all the yuk-yuks we can get here in this cave of despair. Come on, Hank; you're so good at making people laugh!"

"Pleeeeze," Mattie joined in, staring up at him with those pleading eyes. In unison, both the women repeated Mattie's "pleeeeze" and her stare, and Hank knew he'd been suckered in. With a chuckle, he finally agreed.

"Oh, good! We'll pass the word around. How about Wednesday around two o'clock?" Mattie asked. "Is that good for you?"

"Oh . . . okay," he promised, grinning.

The women squealed gratefully and began stopping at some of the residents' doors to let them know.

And Mattie thought to herself: A stand-up comic at Autumn Leaves. Now that's a first!

Mary A. Berger

18

After contacting several of the residents about the upcoming program with Hank, Mattie and Clare returned to their wing and Clare invited her to stop in for a cold drink. Mattie accepted and hurried to beat Clare to Clare's lounge chair, a feat at which they often tried to outdo each other. Giggling, Mattie blurted, "I won!"

Clare let out a disgruntled "huh" and handed Mattie a glass of soda, then flopped on a footstool. Again, Mattie noticed the soda, not Clare's usual belt-of-the-day, but said nothing. If Clare suddenly didn't feel the need for alcohol for reasons Mattie was unaware of, that was Clare's business. She simply accepted Clare the way she was and liked her that way.

Then Clare offered, "I'm trying to cut back, you know, on the sauce."

Mattie nodded and responded by clanking her soda can with Clare's, yet still said nothing.

The women got engrossed in political talk, unusual for them, since they both knew they were at opposite ends of the political spectrum. Being reasonable adults, they made their points in a mature manner.

"He's a bum!" Clare spouted.

"No, Clare. It's the press; they're all against him! Everywhere you look, it's negative. Can't you see that?!"

"That's crazy!

"Well, I think the press is crazy!"

Finally, they reached a stalemate. "I think we should continue this some other time, don't you?" Mattie asked, with a sudden twinkle in her eye.

"Yeah, you're right, Matts. There's no point in arguing, even though I'm right," Clare added under her breath.

Mattie reached for her neck, pretending to strangle her and they both ended up giggling.

"I don't know what I'd do if you weren't here," Mattie confessed to her pal.

"Me, too," Clare answered.

Just then, they heard Scotty in the hall, calling for Mattie. "Anybody seen my aunt?" they heard him ask. "The pretty lady with the gutsy attitude?" And he stuck his head into Clare's room. "I thought I might find you here. I just saw Lauren and thought I'd stop by."

Mattie set her drink down, went to him and they exchanged one of their big hugs. She couldn't remember whether she'd ever introduced him to Clare but did so anyway.

"He's my computer guy—*and* my favorite nephew!" she said, grinning.

Scotty greeted Clare, and said with a smirk, "I'm her only nephew." Looking at Clare, he said, "But you probably already knew that?"

"Um-hmm. I've heard a lot about you Scotty," Clare said, then offered him a cold drink.

"No thanks." He looked at Mattie. "I wanted to check out your computer, if this is a good time."

"Oh, sure, Scotty." She thanked Clare for the drink, said she'd see her around, and she and Scotty went over to Mattie's room.

"Scotty," Mattie told him when they got to her computer. "There's something I've been meaning to tell you." Then she went on about her discovery of the computer and printer in the "mystery" room there at the center.

"You just walked in there?"

"Well, I got confused and thought I was in the ladies' room. The door was unlocked."

"But didn't a little voice tell you to scram out of there?"

Mattie gave a shrug. "Yeah...but since when do I listen to that?"

Scotty shook his head and chuckled. "Aunt Mattie," he said, pretending to scold her. "When will you ever learn?"

"Maybe when I'm old and gray?"

"Seriously, you found records for this joint's spending, and cash being diverted to Reemes and Prescott?" She nodded. "You're sure?"

"I know what I saw." Then Mattie remembered to tell him about the printer, which held the made-up certificates of approval for Autumn Leaves.

Scotty pulled out a chair and sat at Mattie's computer. "Let's see what we can do here." She watched as he pulled down one file after another and one menu after another, while weird looking things were displayed on the monitor screen. She went to make tea and could hear him jabbering to himself and muttering an occasional cuss word. As it turned out, Scotty spent a good part of the afternoon there.

"Aunt Mattie, would you mind if I take some more time? I've got an idea."

"Of course not. I don't know what you're looking for but"

He nodded at her laptop. "Just doing a little 'browsing'," he said with a mischievous grin.

She shrugged. "Breaking into the Pentagon?"

"Something like that. I'll be a while here, so if there's something you need to do"

Mattie decided to step out into the hall, to kill some time, if nothing else. While there, Mr. Reemes and her "friend," the "grudgeful" medic, came by. They both looked worried; their eyes met Mattie's, but they passed by without saying a word. *The alligators look hungry*, she thought.

She did a few stretches, and then paused; her thoughts turning to Jed, and also to what was happening with Eva. She sent up a prayer that Eva would cooperate, and make a confession about what happened. *In your dreams*, she thought, with a smirk.

Finally, she heard Scotty's "ya-hoo!" that could probably be heard as far away as Jean's farm. "Got it!" Next thing Mattie knew, her printer was grinding out some papers. "Is this what you saw in that padlocked room, Aunt Mattie?"

Mattie sucked in a gasp. Upon closer inspection, she saw that the printout was exactly what she'd seen earlier: the current budget for Autumn Leaves, with the misappropriated funds shown under Reemes' and Prescott's travel accounts, and a copy of the certificate of approval they'd apparently concocted to ward off prying busybodies like Mattie.

"Wow, Scotty! How'd you do this?"

"Just need to know a few shortcuts."

"But isn't this illegal?" she asked, her eyes big as melons.

"Uh, maybe a little underhanded," he told her.

"Welcome to the club," she replied.

"Don't worry, Aunt Mattie, there's no way any of this could be traced back to your computer. So why don't you just hang onto these papers. In fact, you might want to show them to Jed next time you see him." He started to clear her computer but ran an extra copy "just to be covered." After deleting everything he'd found, he checked his watch. "Oh, man! I'm gonna be late for Lauren. Look, I've gotta run, Aunt Mattie."

She thanked him for all his work, they exchanged hugs, and he was on his way.

Mattie puzzled over what to do with the printouts. Instinct told her not to leave them lying around. She put one copy in a nightstand drawer that had a lock on it. For some reason, she tucked the other copy inside her jogging suit jacket, on her way to Clare's to see if she wanted to take a stroll.

Clare agreed and along the way they began chatting about Jed and the case. Mattie had filled her in on some of the recent details of what was happening with what little she knew, that is. Over the months, she'd begun to feel closer to Clare and had even opened up to her about the circumstances with Eva.

"I hope they nail that broad," Clare sneered.

Snickering, Mattie said, "I wonder if they picked her up wearing her orange-glow bathing suit that lights up like a beacon for sailors."

Up ahead, Mattie noticed something. It appeared that Mr. Reemes and the medic were carrying equipment outside. She put her hand out in front of Clare. "Wait up, Clare. I don't know what's going on with those two, but I don't like it. Let's stop here a minute."

So the women stood back, unseen, and watched as Jim Reemes handed a computer to the medic. Then Reemes walked out behind him, toting a printer.

Mattie looked thoughtful and muttered, "Now why in the world would they be getting rid of that stuff?" She had already told Clare about what she'd found in the little room that day when it was unlocked.

Clare frowned and turned to Mattie. "It's almost as if someone's on their trail," she said, "and they're ditching evidence."

"Clare, I think you hit the nail right on the head. Maybe they're expecting company," Mattie said, looking thoughtful. "They must know something. And that gives me an idea." As they watched the men leave the building with the door to the "secret" room still ajar, she whispered, "C'mon, Clare."

"What are you doing, Mattie?"

"It's a long shot, but it just might work. Hurry, Clare!" They bolted down the hall to the room. "Watch the door for me!" Mattie whispered as she sneaked inside. Indeed, just as Clare had said, it appeared they were getting rid of evidence. The room was clear!

Mattie saw a small, empty closet. Instinctively, she sped over, reached into her jacket, and took out Scotty's printout. She had no sooner laid it casually on the closet floor, then she heard Clare whisper, "Get outta there, Mattie! They're coming back!"

With lightning speed, Mattie scooted out to the hall, and the women zipped around a corner without being spotted.

"Whew!" Clare wheezed, shaking her head. "Girl, why do I always feel like I'm doing guerrilla warfare when I let you talk me into these things?!" She was panting with one hand to her chest. "Whew!" she repeated.

"I know," Mattie said, breathless, herself. "But look at all the fun we're having!" In a daring moment, she peeked back around the corner to watch Reemes and the medic. They returned to the room, and she saw Reemes lock the door, and then watched as the men hastily left the building. She breathed a huge sigh of relief that they hadn't gone back inside the room.

"They're gone!" she whispered to Clare. Once their breathing had returned to semi-normal, the women started back to their wing. Still visibly shaken, Clare said, "Uh, Mattie, even though I'm trying to cut back on my drinking, don't you think some 'orange juice' might be in order just about now?"

"I'm with you, kid," Mattie replied, one hand on her chest.

In Clare's room, she asked Mattie what this last "adventure" was all about.

"I'm not sure, Clare," Mattie answered. "Just a gut feeling."

"About what?"

"I can't say right now, Clare. Let's just hope my instincts are right." And Clare knew not to push her friend further, and she went to prepare their drinks.

The next day was dull and rainy. Mattie picked up her mystery book and started in where she'd left off. Before long, she dozed off and had a short nap. She awoke to Clare's voice, calling softly to her. "Mattie...hey, Mattie. Wake up."

She frowned and yawned. "Oh, it's you Clare. What's happening?"

Clare came over to her and lowered her voice. "I have an idea that our thinking was right on. There are some official looking people with Mr. Bates outside his office."

"Really?" Mattie hopped out of her chair.

"I thought you'd probably want to see for yourself, Deputy Morgan."

Casually strolling the hall, the two of them approached the hall to Mr. Bates' office. Sure enough, they saw him talking with two men and a woman. It all looked pretty serious. As they approached, Harold called Mattie over.

"I'll wait here," Clare said, while Mattie joined Bates and the others. He introduced her to the people who, it turned out, were from Raleigh, where Bates had reported what Mattie had observed in the "locked room." After speaking with them for a moment, they confided that this was a surprise visit, hopefully to catch things in full operation.

"Let's go check that room for ourselves," one of the men said, and they started for the "mystery room" as Mattie dubbed it.

"It's probably locked," she told them.

Harold agreed. "We'll have to get the key from Jim Reemes." With that, he stopped by Reemes' office but he wasn't there. His desktop appeared neat and orderly—and empty.

"Something's wrong," he muttered. "He's not here," he told the others.

The woman gave a cunning smile. "I'll get us in," she said. Reaching into her satchel, she took out some sort of special key (Mattie assumed), and watched as the woman inserted it into the padlock, then give the door a heavy push. The door opened. "Bingo!" she called out.

One glance inside told the story. The room was empty, as Mattie already knew.

Mattie's mouth dropped open in false shock. "But, but there was a computer and a printer here; I swear, Harold! It was here!"

"I believe you, Mattie." Bates looked dumbfounded as they all stepped inside the room and looked around. Unknown to everyone, Wynn Prescott had somehow gotten word of a surprise visit from Raleigh. He quickly let Jim Reemes know and, naturally, that meant clearing everything out.

While the people from the state were exchanging conversation, Mattie opened the closet door, retrieved the papers, and said with mock surprise, "Well, what's this?" And she handed the printout to one of the men.

"They must've left these behind." he said, gawking. "I'm glad you thought to check that closet, Mrs. Morgan!" And he shook her hand vigorously. "This is just what we need!"

The woman turned to Harold Bates. "I have a feeling we won't be seeing Jim Reemes around here any more, Harold. You know, we've been suspicious of him for some time."

"We're just glad you contacted us," one of the men said.

"I've been trying for months," Harold assured them, shrugging, "but haven't had any luck."

The woman cocked her head and said with authority, "We'll take it from here. And be assured, we'll be on Reemes' trail. And, Harold, would you run Autumn Leaves, at least until we get this mess straightened out? We'll need someone with your character."

"I'll be glad to step in," Bates said enthusiastically. "Maybe I can get Mrs. Morgan here to be my right hand for a while."

Mattie's mouth dropped in surprise, while everyone shook hands all around and the people thanked both Harold and Mattie. They said they'd be in touch, and then turned to leave with the printout tucked inside the woman's satchel.

Once they were gone, Bates turned to Mattie. "Good thinking, to check that closet, Mattie!" he said.

Mattie wore a somewhat mischievous expression. Bates raised one eyebrow suspiciously.

"What?" she said, looking right at him, "haven't you ever heard of dumb luck?"

 19

Mattie heard her telephone ringing as she returned from one of her trips to the greenhouse area. She hurried to answer it before the caller hung up.

"Hello?"

"Oh, Mattie, I'm glad I caught you. It's so great to hear your voice!" It was Jed.

Her face lit up. "It's wonderful to hear from you, Jed. I haven't wanted to call and bother you, but I'm dying to know: What is going on with Eva?"

"That's what I'm calling about. They're bringing her in this afternoon and I think you should be here. I talked to Scotty. He's coming down to pick you up. He has a helper now, so it's a little easier for him to leave his shop.

"Yes, he mentioned something about that the other day."

"Well, it's all arranged. Scotty will be at your place around three, if that's okay with you?"

"Absolutely! I can't wait to see that stepdaughter of mine!"

Jed snickered, and then said softly, "I can't wait to see you." There was a pause, and he said, "I've missed you so much, Mattie. The only thing that keeps me from losing my mind is the knowledge that your case will be finishing up."

"Oh, Jed, that's so nice to hear," she said. "But we have to do what we have to do right now."

"I know...it's just that I can't stop thinking about you."

Mattie could sense that look even over the phone and swallowed hard. "I'll see you later then, Jed," she said, once more with that catch in her voice.

"Yes. Bye, Mattie."

She managed a feeble "good-bye" but didn't think he heard.

Hanging up, she stood looking out her window. Jed's words were just beginning to sink in: "your case will be finishing up." It had been such a long, emotional roller coaster; part of her was afraid to think things would ever be over. She worried that somehow, some way; Eva's evil nature would resurface and spoil things again.

Standing erect, she scolded herself for thinking that way, especially after all Jed had done. She straightened her shoulders and went to her closet. She would choose a nice outfit to wear and show that stepdaughter of hers who she was dealing with. In fact, Mattie wanted to look rather spectacular so Eva wouldn't assume she'd been living the life of a recluse, forced into a pitiful existence. She chose a light blue-grey pants suit with a white "cami" underneath, and her white sandals.

After getting dressed, she glanced at her reflection in a mirror and smiled approvingly. Actually, she looked drop-dead gorgeous, but Mattie was unaware of her own beauty. She felt there were other, more important things to think about.

Scotty arrived on time and they chatted all the way back up to Asheville.

"Aunt Mattie, did anything else happen with that paperwork I dug up for you?"

"Oh, yes!" And then, Mattie related the story of how the people from the state found the locked, empty room, and how she "discovered" Scotty's papers in the closet after sneakily planting them there in the first place.

He nearly drove off the road; he was so intrigued by what she'd told him. "You really should be working for the sheriff!" he spouted.

They arrived at the police station in Asheville and both hurried inside. Jed met them at the door to a small conference room and he and Mattie exchanged a long, warm embrace.

"I've missed you so," he told her again.

"Jed," Scotty asked, "how much have you told Eva?"

Jed snickered. "We've pumped her up with all kinds of stories about Owen Black ratting on her and telling us everything. At this point, she's mad as hell. We'll pit them against each other in a while because we told him the same thing about her. Should be interesting, no?" he said, before adding wickedly, "Ain't it cool?"

An officer came into the room and Jed turned to Mattie. "This is only a casual sort of 'get-together'," he explained. "Nothing formal. I thought things might be easier this way, and the chief agreed."

Chief of Police Bill Weaver was already seated at a conference table. Mattie and Scotty took seats off to one side, and then another officer walked in with Eva at his side. She looked awful, Mattie thought, cringing. Wearing a pair of blue jean cut-offs, a wrinkled brown shirt and flip-flops, her hair hung in strings about her face. Looking like one of those sleep-deprived people in a mattress ad on television, Eva simply sulked and looked straight ahead.

The officers took their seats around the conference table, while Jed started in on Eva. "Well," he said, heaving a big sigh, "here we go again, Eva. What do you have to say for yourself?"

With a smirk, she answered dryly, "I don't know why I'm here."

"We've already talked about that: stealing; falsifying information; and," he added emphatically, "bilking your stepmother out of her estate."

"I told you yesterday: everything was legal," she said, looking up at the ceiling.

Jed looked startled. "And I told you, that's not what Owen Black says. And he's told us plenty."

"He's a liar!" Eva looked as if she wanted to strangle Black, which was, of course, what Jed wanted.

"He gave us just about everything we needed to knowhow it was your idea to steal the wills and other papers from the Morgan safe. Do you want to tell us about that now?"

"There's nothin' to tell!" she snapped.

"Okay. Officer, bring in Owen Black."

One of the officers left the room, and then returned a moment later with Black. Owen looked so ragged; Mattie didn't recognize him at first.

On seeing Eva, he nearly crawled across the table to get to her. "What's wrong with you?! Why are you telling them all that stuff?!"

"I didn't tell 'em anything; it's you and your big mouth that's doing—"

"Wait'll I get my hands on you, you bitch! Dumping me the way you did! You'll regret it"

"No, *you'll* regret it, Mr. Big Shot! Besides, I've still got most of the money, you idiot!"

"I don't think so, Eva," Jed said with a shrewd smile. "Officers, I think it's time to bring in the others." He nodded toward the hall.

There was complete silence as everyone's eyes were on the door. The officer returned, leading in none other than Christine, Jason, Milford, and Sybil.

Astonished at seeing them, Eva nearly jumped out of her chair and cried out, "Christine! Milford! What are you doing here?! Tell them about the stock!"

With her hair pulled back in a ponytail, wearing jeans, a sweatshirt, and the stunning bracelet, Christine looked at Eva with repulsion. "What stock?" she said dryly.

"The Angelite stock we all invested in! Tell them!"

Jed interrupted. "Eva, I'd like you to meet someone." And he motioned for Jason to come over.

"That's Jason, her bodyguard!" Eva exclaimed, completely at a loss to understand what was happening.

"Eva, this is Brian Combs," Jed said quietly. "We're partners at my law firm." And he shook hands with Brian.

"What?! No! He's Christine's bodyguard!" Eva yelled out.

Christine spoke then. "Eva, you're pathetic." She turned to Jed. "She told us everything: how she emptied out her father's safe; how she conned this jerk..." she glared at Owen Black "...into using an old will that left everything to her. We had to get her half sloshed," explained Christine, with a sneer. Then she pulled off the shiny bracelet. "It's all here," she added, handing the bracelet to Jed, who opened the back of it and removed a small tape recorder.

At that, Eva let out a cry of utter disbelief. "No! No!"

Turning back to Eva, Christine said, "There is no *Angelite* stock, Eva. What we showed you that night was just a handful of common, diamond look-alikes." She turned to Jed. "She was so easy, Jed. As long as we kept the Margaritas coming!"

The look on Eva's face was one of fear, horror, and rage, combined. She lit into Christine with a vengeance. "I thought you were my friend!" she shrieked. "You lied to me! You set me up!"

A few low snickers went around the room, and even Owen Black let out a "Duh!" before making one more attempt to get to Eva. "You told them everything?!" he shouted in a rage of contempt. "Why did I ever let you talk me into this?!"

"Eva," Christine said, looking right at her. "You really should be more careful how you spend your money, dear."

The seething Eva sat silently, red-faced, and looking straight ahead.

Jed had to let Eva in on the con. "Sybil and Milford are some friends of mine who just happen to be retired police officers." He smiled over at them. "Christine is their friend, an actress from Key West. When I told them what you'd been up to, they jumped right in, wanting to help."

Eva gave a sneer and sat silently, then.

"Oh, and Eva," Jed added, "you really should be more careful how you choose your friends." He wasn't finished. "By the way, that five hundred grand you 'invested'?" That got

Eva's attention. She glared up at him. "That check was deposited by Christine in a special account and we're in the process of returning it to Mrs. Morgan, even though it's only a part of what she would have received if you two hadn't " His words trailed off and he shook his head in disgust.

When Mattie heard about the money, her mouth dropped open in surprise, and she slumped in the chair. Scotty reached over and put his arm around her.

Eva sat even more red-faced and glaring at Owen Black, while he glared back. If looks could kill, everyone in the room would have been goners. Then, oddly enough, Eva began to cry. "I didn't mean to hurt anyone!" she sobbed, hanging her head.

"I think we've all heard enough," Jed said, "don't you, Chief Weaver?"

The chief then put both Eva and Owen under arrest and the officers led them out. "Judge Murphy said he'd be waiting for us."

Mattie sat slightly dazed along with Scotty. But something inside stirred her and she went over to Jed and spoke quietly to him. They talked for a moment longer and Jed said he'd see if he could speak to Judge Murphy. He then left and caught up with the officers.

Meanwhile, Christine and the others came over to Mattie. "I'm so sorry for what happened to you, Mrs. Morgan," Christine said, while they all shook hands.

"We hated for you to see all that, you know, with Eva," Jed's partner, Brian Combs, told her. "But she conned you and we knew we had to con her. It was the only way."

Still somewhat in shock, Mattie introduced Scotty, and then thanked them all for their part in everything.

"We did it for Jed, too," Brian said. "He's the best, and I feel privileged to be his partner."

Mattie nodded. The thought of what Jed had told her about turning his practice over to Brian and becoming a consultant flashed through her mind, and she wondered if Brian had been told about it yet.

Stepping back into the room, Jed answered the question for her. "I'd like to take a moment to let you all know I'm going to be easing out of my practice, just doing a little consulting work now and then, and Brian, here, will be taking over." And Jed looked fondly at Mattie with a sly grin.

Obviously, Brian already knew about Jed's plans. He was beaming as the two of them shook hands. "I can only hope we don't get another case like this one," Brian said, pretending to wipe his brow. "That woman is something else!"

They shook hands all around and exchanged congratulations. As they broke up, Christine reassured Mattie that the money Mattie was so deserving of was in the process of being transferred and would be in Jed's hands in a few days.

It was past dinnertime when Mattie, Scotty, and Jed got back out to their cars. "I'll run Mattie back, Scotty," Jed told him.

"Hey, I think we need to celebrate, don't you?" Scotty asked, his face full of happiness for his aunt.

"Why don't we pick up some pizza and soda and all come back to my place?" Mattie said; she hated to miss a party and this was the perfect time for her to host her own. "We have to celebrate!" Jed handed Scotty some cash and asked if he'd mind picking up the snacks.

"Hey, no problem," said Scotty. "You da man!"

Mattie and Jed exchanged a long embrace when they reached his car.

"It's over!" said Jed, excitedly, as they both slid inside the car.

"I knew you'd take care of everything," she told him, beaming. "I just knew it!"

During the drive back to Autumn Leaves, they sat silently for the most part, while the day's events began to sink in. Every now and then, they exchanged glances, grinning like school kids.

"Jed, how did you do all that with the others, I mean?" She looked puzzled. "I can't even begin to comprehend it!"

Jed gave her a sneaky smile. "Sometimes, you have to think like the bad guys."

When they finally reached the center and started inside, Mattie heard someone calling to her from across the hall. She couldn't believe her eyes, when she saw Fae Munn slowly and deliberately pushing a walker! Lauren was at her side. Fae pointed down into a basket that was attached to the front of the walker. Sitting inside it and perched regally like a king sat Scooter, who wagged his tail, happy to see Mattie.

She introduced Mae to Jed and they chatted briefly, while petting the dog. Lauren was all smiles when Mattie told her about the outcome of the proceedings at the courthouse. Then Lauren said she should get Fae back to her room. "Don't want to overdo our first outing," she told Fae warmly. Of course, Mattie invited Lauren to come back to her room where the celebration was about to begin.

Scotty had arrived at Mattie's and when she and Jed got there, Clare was inside giving him a hand with the pizza. "Matts!" Clare cried out, rushing over to give her and Jed a huge hug. "I'm so happy for you! What an ordeal you've been through!" Then with a wide grin, she added, "But it's over now and you can put that slut of a stepdaughter out of your mind!" And with that, she went around pouring champagne for everyone.

Just then, Lauren stepped into the room and she and Scotty exchanged a short kiss.

Jed cleared his throat and gave a call for attention. "I have some news for all of you," he said, in charge, and sounding lawyerly. "After speaking with Judge Murphy at the courthouse, he's decided that he'll go a little easy on

Eva; she'll probably only have to serve a short time, but after that he has sentenced her to community service for one year, doing housekeeping duties...here at Autumn Leaves!"

A round of cheers and hoots and tapping of champagne glasses took place as everyone heard Jed's news. Mattie grinned at him, while everyone began digging into the pizza Clare was cutting.

Harold Bates even showed up. "Oh, Mattie, you missed Hank this afternoon," he told her, helping himself to a slice of pizza. "You were right about him. He's funny! At first there were only four or five people in the lobby, but little by little more folks showed up, and before long the whole lobby was filled!"

"Imagine" Clare added, "people were actually laughing out loud! Here at Autumn Leaves! Doesn't that fire up your meatballs!"

Lauren joined right in. "Yeah, I couldn't catch all of it, but from what I heard, he was a hoot! Everyone seemed to enjoy it."

"That's great," Mattie said, beaming. "Maybe he'll do another program sometime."

Mattie glanced at the door and to her surprise she saw Harry, the odd mail clerk who'd supplied her with the contraband markers and paper. "Come in, Harry!" she called to him.

He held one hand out. "No, no, Miss Mattie. No time to stop. I was just wondering how them little young 'uns of yours were doing?"

The party came to a screeching halt, and Mattie knew she'd been caught. She swallowed a big gulp of her drink as Scotty let out a catcall and the others followed suit with "oohs" and hoots of teasing. Even Harold Bates joined in.

"Why, Mattie," he said, feigning surprise, "I never realized you had little ones!"

Mattie came right back and said, straight-faced, "I try to keep it quiet."

More hoots followed from Scotty, and the two of them got into another one of their hand slapping battles, while the others looked on, cheering. Meanwhile, Harry the mail clerk shrugged and walked away, bewildered.

Everyone stayed at Mattie's throughout the evening, chatting, and having a good time. It was after ten o'clock when the party broke up. "I'm so happy you were all here," she told them as they began to leave. She had kicked off her shoes, removed her jacket, and was thanking everyone for their good wishes.

Clare hung around to help clean up, and finally she told Mattie that was the latest she'd stayed up since they went on their midnight "dirty work" mission distributing the flyers.

At last, when everyone had left, Jed and Mattie had the place all to themselves. He took her in his arms. "You never gave up on me, did you Mattie?"

She smiled up at him. "Of course not. You told me to hang in there, so I did." He reached across her shoulder and turned off the light, and she sighed, "It's all over, Jed! I'm so thankful." She patted her eyes with a tissue.

"Yes, it's finally over." They slumped into each other with relief. Then he took her by the hand and led her over to the open window where they stood together. "Let's look at the stars," he said, enfolding her in his arms.

Both silent, they felt the sultry, summer breeze wrap itself around them. Jed's warm smile met hers. "Mattie, Mattie," he whispered softly, his cheek brushing against her hair. "It's wonderful seeing you so happy." They made a striking silhouette, their arms encircling each other, their bodies locked together in the near-darkened room, with only a slight trace of moonlight peeking in at the window, and the katydids chirping their love calls in the distance.

Jed was softly caressing her back with his strong hands, and she pressed her face to his chest.

Out of the blue, he said abruptly, "Mattie, let's get married." Then he said softly, "Say you'll marry me?"

She inhaled deeply. "When?!"

"Tomorrow."

"Tomorrow?! Oh, how wonderful! But—"

"Shhhh. Everything's taken care of."

"How, Jed?"

"I'm a lawyer, Mattie. We take care of things." His breathing was heavy as he drew her even closer, stroking her back and speaking between kisses to her cheek. "I was so hoping you'd say yes that I talked to an old judge friend today. He has a small wedding chapel and told me we could come by his place tomorrow morning . . ."

"Tomorrow morning?! Oh, Jed," she whispered, close to tears of joy. "I must be in Heaven!"

"Mattie," his voice was low and earthy, "I want to be with you every day for the rest of my life." He spoke just above a whisper, as he kissed her shoulder. "You know I want you more than anything in this world. Say you'll marry me?"

She could almost make out that look, and melted in his arms again. "Yes, Jed; yes, I'll—" His lips were on hers then, warm, tender, moist, and so enticing.

"I love you, dear Mattie," he murmured, his touch gentle and natural, his breath warm and sensuous on her skin; "I think I've loved you forever."

She whispered back breathlessly, "And I love you, Jed."

220

The agony of the past months disappeared in that tender moment, as their pent-up emotions poured out. Then, with little regard for time or place, and with hearts as one, they loved deeply—and passionately —into the night.

Mary A. Berger

20

The next morning, Mattie woke to her phone ringing. "Hello," she answered sleepily.

"Are you as happy as I am?"

"Jed," she murmured, beaming. "I couldn't be happier."

"I'll be there in about an hour. I love you, Mattie."

"I love you more."

They hung up and the utterly happy Mattie showered quickly, dabbed on a little make-up, and then slipped into her pink suit and white sandals. Then she rushed over to Clare's and pounded on her door. "Clare, open up! It's me, Mattie."

Clare came to the door, still in her pajamas, and frowning. "What now, Matts?" she asked, squinting at her pal.

"We're getting married, Clare! I need you as a witness. Come on, get dressed! We don't have much time!"

"Huh?" Clare responded dumbly.

"You heard me," Mattie said, grinning. "Jed and I are getting married this morning, in about two hours! You'll be our witness, won't you Clare, pleeeeze?"

Clare frowned and shrugged. "Enough with the eyes, Mattie. Don't do that." Then it struck her what Mattie had said, and her sleepy eyes popped open. "You're *what?!* You're getting *married?* OMG!" she shrieked, wide awake then. "What'd they put in that pizza?!"

Mattie giggled and they both exchanged a quick hug. "Be ready in fifteen minutes!" Mattie ordered.

Once more, like the obedient child, Clare quickly tossed her PJs onto the bed, and then went to get dressed.

She met Mattie in fifteen minutes and they scooted out to Jed's waiting car.

"'Mornin', young lady," Jed greeted Clare. "Are you ready for this?"

"Do I have any choice?" she said with her usual good-natured sarcasm, sliding into the back seat.

Jed and Mattie exchanged a long kiss. With the sun shining brightly (just for them, Mattie was certain) they went right to the county clerk's office, took care of the license, for which Jed had already made arrangements, then headed for the little white wedding chapel somewhere in the hills beyond Autumn Leaves. With the judge's wife and Clare acting as witnesses, Jed presented the marriage certificate. Reaching into his pocket, then, he placed a delicate but stunning gold wedding band he'd bought weeks ago on Mattie's finger, while the smiling judge conducted the ceremony.

"I now pronounce you man and wife, Mr. and Mrs. Jed Mitchell!"

Jed and Mattie kissed tenderly, and then they all hugged and thanked the judge and his wife, while Clare and Mattie hugged joyfully.

"I'm so happy for you, Matts," Clare told her, tears streaming down her face.

"Lord above," Mattie said, "I'm so happy myself, I'm raining tears!"

They stopped for a late brunch at a cozy inn in Hendersonville, where everyone ordered the quiche of the day.

Afterwards, as Jed returned to the back roads, with all their twists and turns, Mattie asked, "Jed, I wonder how in the world Eva found Autumn Leaves?"

"Well, I think she had some help. You knew Owen Black and Jim Reemes were pals, didn't you?" Mattie was flabbergasted and shook her head as Jed went on. "Oh, yes; they go back a long time, from what I've heard."

"Well, that explains it then." Mattie was looking out the window, watching the rolling hills pass by. "It's really pretty country, isn't it, Jed?"

"I love it!" he said enthusiastically. "Maybe we could build a place here?"

She reached over and squeezed his arm. "If you're that crazy about it, Jed, so am I!" She peeked at Clare who was grinning in the back seat.

They finally arrived back at Autumn Leaves. When they went inside, Jed and Mattie received a surprise. A table had been set up which held a decorated cake, surrounded by some punch, paper plates and cups. Most of the residents were circled about, all expressing their wishes for the happy couple. Harold Bates was there; Fae Munn with her walker; Lillian; Kathy; Clint; Hank; and many of those who'd attended Mattie's last rally; all were gathered around.

"What's this?!" Mattie exclaimed, one hand over her heart. "Who told you?"

"Word gets around, Mrs. Mitchell." It was Lauren, who came over and fondly embraced Mattie with a huge hug, then explained that Jed had called her early that morning while he was waiting for Mattie to come out to the car. "We really had to do some fast work to pull this off!" she said, grinning.

"How wonderful!" Mattie was glowing, while Lauren and Clare began cutting the cake and filling cups with punch.

As they were finishing, Harold Bates came over to Mattie, looking smug. "You look sneaky, Harold," she told him. "What're you up to?"

"This," he said, turning to Hank. Hank had brought in a large sign. When Mattie stepped back to read it, she saw that it said Mattie's Retreat. "We all got together and decided Autumn Leaves sounded like some old fogey's place," Harold said. "It's our new sign and it's going up in place of that old thing outside." He nodded toward the entrance, and then placed his hand on Mattie's. "It's just our way of saying thanks for all you've done for everyone here."

Mattie stood speechless, as humble tears of appreciation filled her eyes. "This is...so nice," she said weakly. "I can't tell you how much—" Clare was on the spot with a tissue, and Mattie wiped her eyes. "It's wonderful!" Mattie said, and then went around thanking each of them.

"Mattie," Lillian called over to her, "about our greenhouse. We're off to such a good start, but we need you to keep us going. I think you should plan some workshops out there or something. We'd like to start a community garden, where everyone has their own area. How's that sound?"

"I like that idea!" Mattie said. "So you go ahead and get things lined up and somehow, some way I'll be back to help." She looked up lovingly at Jed. "But not for a while."

226

He gave her an affectionate squeeze and nodded in agreement, then kissed her on the cheek.

It was then Mattie noticed Clare wasn't around. "Where'd Clare disappear to?" she asked Lauren.

"Probably had to use the bathroom," Lauren said quietly with a snicker.

After a while, there still was no sign of Clare. "I'm going looking for her," Mattie told Jed.

"Hurry back," he said, with his special look.

Mattie nodded and gave a low "whew!" as she turned away. She started down the hall but paused at Clare's room before knocking. She thought she heard something. Yes, it was Clare and it sounded like she was crying. With a short tap on the door, Mattie opened it slowly. She saw Clare sitting on her bed. "Clare, what's wrong?" Mattie asked full of concern. She went right over to her and sat beside her. "What is it, Clare?"

Clare gave a sniff, then dabbed her eyes. "Mattie, I'm really happy for you, you know that, don't you?" Mattie nodded. "It's just that you and I have gotten to be such good friends and I'm going to miss you. I mean, I've never had so much fun with anyone in my life as I've had with you. We just seem to click in sort of an unusual way," she added, giggling, then.

"Aw, Clare," Mattie said affectionately, giving her pal a squeeze.

"Now you'll be gone and I'm afraid things will go back to the way they were before you came here." And she broke down again.

Momentarily, Mattie was at a loss for words. Finally, she said, "Clare, I have to admit I've grown to love you like a sister. And I've got something I need to tell you. I've never had so much fun with anyone in my life, either!" The two women embraced, half giggling, half sobbing. "But there's something else I need to tell you," Mattie said, sniffling.

"What?"

"I've already talked to Jed about it and after we come back from our honeymoon, he wants me to continue with some of the things I've started here. He's probably going to be a

little busy with his consulting work, anyway, and you heard him say he wants to live down here! So we'll have to be looking to build or relocate somewhere in this area."

"Oh, that's nice."

"And there's something else," Mattie went on. "You knew that Harold Bates has been put in charge here at the center, didn't you? Well, he wants me to give him a hand with some things, and do you know what I told him?"

"What?"

"I said I'd help him only if my partner in crime could join me. And that's you. So what do you say, girl, are you in?" She looked tearfully and pitifully into Clare's eyes. "Pleeeeze?"

With a sniffle, Clare smiled and replied, "Do I have any choice?"

 The End

Epilogue

Mattie and Jed went on to buy a lovely new home not far from the center. Despite talking about having a home built, they both fell in love with a Mediterranean style classic with its four bedrooms, one of which Jed would use for his office, and a gorgeous, sunny, garden room, where Mattie's plants would thrive. Flanked by large pillars at the entrance, the home faces the mountains with a spectacular view of Mt. Pisgah.

Jed still gives Mattie "that look," and she still melts. After they got settled, they opened their home for a huge wedding reception, and included all their friends. Scotty and Lauren announced their engagement, to Mattie's delight. Jed's consulting work sometimes takes him to other parts of the country, but only for short trips. Mattie frequently returns to the center, where she and Clare work together and like to refer to themselves as the "git-'er-done girls." But their work is "just the beginning," according to Mattie; there are still so many more "adventures" ahead, she says.

If you're ever out driving along the back roads of western North Carolina, you might come across Mattie's Retreat. It's still there. To find it, head south out of Asheville, go past Mountain Home, head west using the old short cut, then follow the winding road, drive right through Farmer Tom's pasture, unless the gates are closed, in which case he'll tell you: go ahead and open them, then drive on through. Just watch out for the wild turkeys, they don't always know where the pasture ends and the road begins. When you get to the other side of the pasture, take a right at the fork in the road, keep on going, and you'll find Mattie's Retreat up ahead just before you get to Jean's farm.

Or, if you prefer Mattie's way, just head for the moon and take a left.

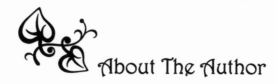

About The Author

A native of Michigan, where she earned her arts degree, Mary A. Berger is an award-winning author whose writing has appeared in The Saturday Evening Post, Ladies' Circle, and Today's Family, as well as in various small-press publications and her local newspaper, the Times-News.

She currently occupies her time with the Friends of Henderson County Public Library, her homeowners association, her pottery, and her church. Married fifty-two years, Mary has two daughters, four grandchildren, and two "greats."

And, yes, she plans to write more adventures for Mattie. Stay tuned. Readers interested in sharing their observations may reach the author via email at: ohminc@bellsouth.net.

Mary A. Berger